the R
of

Sabrina bristled. ' ..aves a bit
to be desired,'' she ..swered, scowling. "I'm
Sabrina Caide. I own the marina."

"I know." He finished filling out his registration
form and looked up again. "Chase Cutter," he
announced, as though the name itself were sufficient
introduction.

"I know." Sabrina took a small amount of
satisfaction in mimicking his confident response.
Then a slow smile touched his lips, and she had the
impression that her words had only acknowledged a
reputation he knew to be formidable. What was
more, she sensed that it pleased him.

BEVERLY BIRD

makes her home in Arizona, though she spent most of
her life on a small island off the coast of New Jersey.
She is devoted to both her husband and her writing,
but still makes time for travel and horseback riding.

Dear Reader:

SILHOUETTE DESIRE is an exciting new line of contemporary romances from Silhouette Books. During the past year, many Silhouette readers have written in telling us what other types of stories they'd like to read from Silhouette, and we've kept these comments and suggestions in mind in developing SILHOUETTE DESIRE.

DESIREs feature all of the elements you like to see in a romance, plus a more sensual, provocative story. So if you want to experience all the excitement, passion and joy of falling in love, then SILHOUETTE DESIRE is for you.

For more details write to:

Jane Nicholls
Silhouette Books
PO Box 236
Thornton Road
Croydon
Surrey CR9 3RU

BEVERLY BIRD
The Best Reasons

Silhouette Desire

Originally Published by Silhouette Books
division of
Harlequin Enterprises Ltd.

*First published in Great Britain 1985
by Mills & Boon Ltd, 15–16 Brook's Mews, London W1A 1DR*

© Beverly Bird 1985

Silhouette, Silhouette Desire and Colophon are Trade Marks
of Harlequin Enterprises B.V.

ISBN 0 373 05190 5

22-0885

*Made and printed in Great Britain by
Richard Clay (The Chaucer Press) Ltd,
Bungay, Suffolk*

For Steve, with all my love,
in memory of Chub Cay
and the "Orient Express"

The Best
Reasons

1

~∞∞∞∞∞∞∞∞~

She was almost exactly what he'd expected.

Chase Cutter kept a surreptitious eye on the woman coming out of the marina restaurant as he passed along the nearby pier on his way to the office. He had, in fact, been keeping an eye on her from the time he had first guided his yacht, the *Amazing Grace,* into the harbor some twenty minutes earlier. She was the tiny Bahamian island's chief attraction, not only for him but for hundreds of boaters who had sailed into the Thunder Cay marina before him. He'd heard her name bandied about in marinas on half a dozen other islands as he'd cruised through the Bahamas during the last several months. Now he was going to meet the woman behind the rumors. He was looking forward to it. The stories he'd heard about her intrigued him.

She hesitated on the patio as she came out of the restaurant, shielding her eyes against the sun with one hand as she glanced first out at the *Amazing Grace,* then back at him. As Cutter paused on the pier to watch her, the beginnings of a devilish grin touched his lips. She was a captivating sight.

The wind whipped her straight, satiny black hair and molded her loose-fitting white jeans to her slender legs and trim hips. She was tall, probably five foot eight or nine, with coltish long legs, a narrow waist and jutting breasts. And she was wildly beautiful. He'd heard that, of course, from other boaters who had mused about her, but he'd still been unprepared for those fiery dark eyes, high, exotic cheekbones, and the full mouth that was almost pouty.

Abruptly, as though she knew he was assessing her, Sabrina Caide whirled on her heel and disappeared back into the restaurant. It had to be him, she thought. The man sauntering into the office with the almost arrogant stride could be none other than Chase Cutter. First of all, his yacht was unmistakable. It was awesome in its perfection. She hadn't been able to see the transom to catch the name as it came in, but how many Cheoy Lee sixty-six-foot long-range motor yachts were cruising the Bahamas this winter? And she had heard some of the other boaters gossiping in the last few weeks, had known that Cutter and his *Amazing Grace* were heading north toward Thunder Cay. The people who spent winters cruising the islands tended to be a tight clique. They kept tabs on men like Cutter. His reputation and whereabouts had been fodder for a good many cocktail hours. Those at her marina had been no exception.

She was no exception, she thought, stepping behind the bar to fix herself a cold soft drink. To her chagrin, she found that she was just as curious about him as the other men and women who had crowded around this same bar tossing his name back and forth had been. She leaned closer to the plate glass window behind the rows of liquor to peer outside. Cutter crossed the gravel lot between the restaurant and the office, pulled open the door and stepped inside as she watched. When he was out of sight, Sabrina unconsciously let out her breath on a long, shaky sigh.

Chase Cutter was on her island. And from the looks of things, he was everything everyone had said he was. In all of her thirty years, no one had ever looked at her in quite the way he had when he had been walking along the pier toward the office. His gaze had been piercing and contemplative. She might as well have been naked, she thought. And that smile! So smug, so cheerfully wicked! He had smiled at her as though he could read her mind and knew all her secret thoughts and fantasies. As though he believed that reading her mind was within the realm of his capabilities. As though he believed that *anything* was within the realm of his capabilities.

She shivered softly in the air conditioning of the empty bar, drained her glass and moved away from the window. Before she realized what she was doing, she found herself back at the door. Two could play his game, she thought. She could size him up as well as he could her. She yanked open the door and stepped determinedly outside into the brilliant Caribbean sunlight. She had every reason to be in the office when he signed in, she assured herself. He was on her island, docked at her marina.

Besides, she was incredibly curious about the infamous Chase Cutter.

He was leaning against the counter, filling out the

required paperwork for the boat slip he would take, when she entered. He didn't look up at the sound of the little bell tinkling over the door, which announced her arrival. Most people did, she thought. It was human nature to want to see who was behind you. Obviously it wasn't Cutter's nature. Sabrina filed away another impression of arrogance as she slipped through the door next to the counter to move around behind it.

He finally looked up as she passed in front of him. For a moment she was startled into stillness by his eyes. Silver gray and scrutinizing, they captured hers and held them as he smiled slowly. She thought they were the color of lightning.

"You must be the renowned recluse of Thunder Cay," he observed in a quiet yet somehow rough voice. Then his eyes released her, going back to the paperwork in front of him.

Belatedly, Sabrina bristled. It seemed to take several seconds for the air to return to her lungs after his eyes left her. She realized that she had been holding her breath. "Your choice of words leaves a bit to be desired," she answered, scowling. "I'm Sabrina Caide. I own the marina."

"I know." He finished signing his name to a registration form and looked up again. "Chase Cutter," he announced, as though the name itself were sufficient introduction.

"I know." Sabrina took a small amount of satisfaction in mimicking his confident response. Then another slow smile touched his lips, and she had the impression that her words had only acknowledged a reputation he already knew to be formidable. What was more, she sensed that it pleased him. She turned away from him briskly and pulled open a filing cabinet, grabbing the first file she came to without even looking at it. She only hoped that it wasn't one that the office staff would be needing later. She'd feel like a fool trying to explain why she had taken it.

"You'll have to excuse me," she went on tightly. "I have work to do."

He didn't respond as she hurried outside again, but she had the distinct impression that if she had looked over her shoulder at him, she would have found an amused grin on his face. Except men like Cutter didn't generally grin, she thought, heading toward her apartment at the other end of the motel complex. Men like Cutter smiled slowly and self-assuredly, just the way he had. They were suave and convinced of their machismo. Egotistical, her mind raced on. Shallow. They went through women the way Sherman had gone through Georgia. Men like Cutter were exactly the kind she had left the States years before to avoid. She had had her fair share of them, and she detested them.

His reputation fit him like a glove, she decided. He *was* fascinatingly handsome in a craggy, tough sort of way, with his dark, carelessly windblown hair and those eyes the color of steel. She could understand how women would be hopelessly attracted to him. He was tall, but he moved gracefully, like a panther ready to pounce on its prey. There was something sexy about that. She found that she had no trouble at all believing the stories about the notches in his bedpost now that she had met him.

"They were right."

Sabrina nearly stumbled over her own feet at the

sound of his voice. She'd been so lost in her thoughts that she hadn't heard him come up behind her. She spun around to find that he had followed her out of the office and down the graveled walkway instead of using the pier, which would have taken him more directly to the *Amazing Grace*. Oh God, she thought suddenly. With all the women vacationing on Thunder Cay, could he be setting his sights on *her?* Did he work that quickly? An almost forgotten kind of panic fluttered in her stomach. She was not about to become his paramour for this particular port. He'd have to burnish his reputation elsewhere.

Still, her curiosity prodded her into answering him. That, and a certain sense of propriety that came with being the owner of the place. She could hardly ignore the man. "Who was right?" she asked, hesitating on the walkway. He caught up to her within seconds.

"The rumormongers who said you were a beautiful recluse." His eyes slid down her body with cocky assurance.

"I didn't care for your choice of words back in the office, and I don't like it anymore now," she told him defensively. "I don't know where you've been picking up your rumors, but I think you ought to find another source. They're all wrong."

"Are they?" he countered smoothly, then pointed out, "You're beautiful."

Sabrina felt herself flushing. She knew his words were nothing more than a polished come-on, but she couldn't help herself. "I'm certainly not a recluse, though. And I don't know here you got such an idea." Feeling uncomfortable, she nodded toward his yacht and tried to change the subject. "I'm sure Dwight explained to you about the water hookups and whatnot when you were in the office. Is there anything else you need to know?''

"Why you're running off to hide?" he suggested.

"Hide?" she echoed, amazed at his audacity. "I'm not doing any such thing! What's more, I can't imagine where you got an impression like that."

"Recluses do those things," he persisted.

Temper flared within her before she could tell herself that she would only be encouraging him by responding in any way. "Has anyone ever told you that you're obnoxious?" she snapped.

He grinned. Even white teeth flashed briefly against his deep tan. "Often, but they're generally wrong. I just figured that if getting you angry was a way to keep you from running off, it was worth a try."

Oh, yes, he was suave, all right. But then, from what she'd heard, he'd had a lot of practice. She gave him an icy smile. "It was a clever ploy, but I'm afraid it's not going to work. I've got no choice but to run off," she lied. "I've got business to take care of. But just for the record, you might want to set those rumormongers straight when you see them. I'm not a recluse. In fact, I'm just the opposite. Running this place enables me to meet more new people on a day-to-day basis than most people can only dream of. It also enables me to pick and choose the ones I want to associate with. You're not one of them."

Amused surprise showed in his eyes before they became even more blatantly appreciative than before. Sabrina started walking again, more decisively this time. On impulse she changed direction and headed down toward the pier. She decided that she'd go to the customs and immigrations office rather than to her apartment.

15

She knew that she was probably feeling unduly paranoid about him, but she didn't want him to know where she lived.

She sensed more than knew for sure that he was following her again. She could feel the little hairs on the back of her neck prickle as though she were a frightened animal caught in the glaring eyes of a hawk. Well, the situation wasn't really all that different, she thought. He was a womanizer and she was a woman—one who didn't want to be caught.

He was beside her again in no time. Her nerves began singing as he kept pace with her in silence. Sabrina darted a few furtive glances at him from beneath lowered lashes. Why didn't he say anything? What kind of game was he playing with her now?

His silence was worse than his shallow flattery. She couldn't stand it any longer. As they neared his yacht and her eyes took in the name painted across the transom, she blurted, "*Amazing Grace.* Was she?"

A smile had been hovering on his lips as they walked, and now she saw it widen. "Definitely," he answered. "Oh, yes, Grace was definitely amazing."

His unabashed response startled Sabrina into stopping again. She hadn't expected him to be so blatant about his conquests.

"Well," she muttered uncomfortably, "at least you give credit where credit is due. She must have stood a head above all the rest if you named your yacht after her."

Cutter laughed good-naturedly. It was a sound that seemed to come from a deep, dark spot inside him. "First of all," he said eventually, "a sixty-six-foot Cheoy Lee isn't just a yacht."

er that to be one of the best decisions I've ever made. I've never been very interested in metropolises and I'm happy here. Your rumors are true only in the respect that, yes, I'm single—thankfully so—and yes, I live here. The next time you have the urge to discuss me with anyone, I'd appreciate it if you'd delete all references to cloistering or hiding."

He was smiling at her. He didn't seem to be at all perturbed by her anger. For that matter, he didn't seem to be impressed with anything she had said. "Your life here is unnatural," he answered.

"By whose standards?"

"Mine."

"You're a fine one to pass judgment!" she snapped heatedly.

"You've been listening to rumors again," he returned. It infuriated her that his smile never wavered while she was getting hotter and hotter under the collar.

"In your case, it's more reputation than rumors," she pointed out irritably.

"Does it make a difference? There's such a fine line between the two. For instance, rumor has it that you're running from a disastrous love affair—"

"That's asinine!" she exploded. "I hadn't been involved with anyone for years before I came down here."

"That doesn't matter either," he went on unperturbedly. "The point is that you're the mystery lady of Thunder Cay, and that you've been feeding those rumors about yourself simply by staying here and rarely offering anyone any information about yourself. I, on the other hand, am supposedly the Don Juan of the high seas because—"

"Supposedly?" she echoed sarcastically.

She was rewarded only with his impossibly dauntless grin. "Don't be catty," he scolded her. "Just think about it. We're both reacting the same way by keeping our mouths shut about the rumors that chase us and going our merry ways. You ignore them and continue to live here alone. I ignore them and continue to sail the Bahamas every winter with occasional female companionship. So who's to say which of us has the reputation and which of us is the victim of rumors? We're birds of a feather whether you want to admit it or not."

She didn't. What was more, she hated his logic. She felt trapped by it, and more than a little threatened. "I'm *not* running from a disastrous love affair," she insisted again. "You *are* the Don Juan of the high seas, as you so aptly put it. Since rumor implies speculation, and reputation implies truth, I'd say the issue is really pretty clear-cut."

He was laughing at her again. A low, chuckling sound prefaced his words. "And how do you know that I 'am the Don Juan of the high seas'?" he asked, mimicking her exasperated tone of voice.

"I've heard—" she began, then bit off the rest of her words. She ducked her head in embarrassment. Damn him! He'd been baiting her—and loving every minute of it.

"I rest my case," he replied smoothly. "And actually, just for the record, I haven't been involved with half the women I've been linked with. I only wish I had been." Humor touched his words, but it didn't eradicate the ring of honesty he finished with. He *enjoys* his reputation! she thought again.

She turned away from him. She could still feel his eyes on her, but she didn't look at him. She didn't want to see the laughter or indomitable self-assurance in his eyes. Her gaze swept over the *Amazing Grace* again as she kept her back to him, trying once more to find words that would offer her a polite escape.

But the slender, bronzed legs that appeared at the top of the ladder to the fly bridge at that moment dashed any such thoughts for Sabrina. She watched, her dark eyes wide and surprised, as bikini-clad hips joined the legs. A moment later they were followed by a slim, tanned torso and lush breasts barely confined by a scrap of bikini top. The stunning blonde tossed a strand of long hair over her shoulder and offered Sabrina a bland smile of greeting before she disappeared into the salon.

Sabrina whirled around to face Cutter again. He was grinning even more widely now.

"For someone who hasn't been involved with half the women you've been linked with, you're not doing too badly for yourself," she observed dryly. As soon as the words were out, she regretted them.

Cutter laughed uproariously. "Sorry. I'd love to feed the fire of my reputation, but I can't take credit for her. Marci's on board with her husband. Whatever else you've heard about me, I leave married women alone. Sorry to disappoint you. I'm doing this cruise *sans* female companionship. Although," he mused, and she had the sense that he was only pretending to think aloud, "you can't blame me for hoping that that state of affairs will change."

His eyes were still laughing at her. She might have tolerated that, but beneath the laughter she saw something more. His gaze was a quicksilver flash of promise. It set her senses reeling and her heart skidding into an unnatural rhythm. A dam exploded inside her and flooded her with defensive panic almost as old as she was.

"Not here it won't change," she snapped darkly. "There aren't a hell of a lot of available women on Thunder Cay right now, much less willing ones. I hate to break this to you, Cutter, but you're going to find slim pickings on this island."

His smile softened. When he answered, warning bells began to ring violently inside her.

"It doesn't matter," he murmured. "I've already picked."

2

⸺∾⦁⦁⦁⦁⦁⦁⦁⦁⦁⦁⦁⦁∾⸺

Sabrina took two steps onto the patio outside the restaurant before she stopped abruptly. Her gaze skipped warily over the boaters congregated there for breakfast. Nothing, she thought dismally, was as it should have been.

She didn't own the island itself, but she owned a large part of it—the land the marina complex was situated on as well as the marina itself. It had been her oasis for nearly two years. It was a haven for her, a place where life had always been predictable and peaceful.

But it wasn't predictable any longer. It hadn't been predictable since Chase Cutter had cruised into the harbor the day before. For the first time since she had come to Thunder Cay, she felt wired and uptight. She wasn't even able to have breakfast without first stopping to see if the man had beaten her to it and was already on the patio.

She moved to a table and sat down, then caught the eye of one of the waiters. Giving him a nod and a smile to indicate that she wanted to eat, she settled back in her chair with a ragged sigh to wait for her usual breakfast of ham and eggs.

She could scarcely believe that Cutter had set his sights on *her*. But there seemed to be no doubt about it, not after what he had said yesterday about having picked his latest conquest. My God! she thought. I feel like a hunted animal! It shouldn't be that way, not here, not on my own island! She thought she'd left all that back in the States with Ken!

She had to find a way to avoid Cutter while he was here, she thought emphatically. She couldn't go through all that again; she—

Her thoughts stumbled to a standstill. Just as she glanced up at the waiter who delivered her breakfast, she caught sight of Cutter out of the corner of her eye. He had jumped down onto the pier from the *Amazing Grace* and was heading toward the restaurant.

She wouldn't run. Damn it, she wouldn't! This was her island, her turf! She wasn't going to allow a man like him to disrupt her life again. Her fingers tightened around her water glass as she closed her eyes and took a deep, steadying breath. She was vaguely surprised at the depth of the panic that kicked through her. But it had its roots. . . . God knew it had its roots.

Never again, she thought, her eyes flying open once more. She'd paid her dues with men like Cutter. All those months she had spent trying to avoid Ken . . . Ken with his chocolate eyes and his candy-coated flattery. The more she had tried to avoid getting emotionally tangled up with him, the more persistently he had pursued her. Oh, they were of the same ilk, Ken and Cutter. Brazen, handsome, charming. They had the same knack of telling lies with a ring of truth. After listening to them long enough, you almost had to start believing them. Early on she had known that Ken wanted nothing more than for her to be something pretty and successful to drape over his arm. He wanted the money and the notoriety she had earned for herself during those grueling years when her face had adorned all those magazine covers. But eventually he had made her forget all that. Eventually he had convinced her to marry him. And within months she had realized that she had been right about him all along. He wanted her face in the advertisements for his restaurants. He wanted to know all the right people she could introduce him to at his parties. And he wanted any other woman he could get his hands on in his bed.

God, how people had talked! He had made no secret of his roaming, had even led people to believe that she did the same thing herself. She'd had no choice but to leave Houston when Ken had finished with her reputation—and she had finished with their marriage.

The man had disrupted her life in an enormous way. But she'd learned a lesson. She'd never trust anyone like him again. She'd never let another man like him get close to her. She wasn't going to go through that again. She was going to put Cutter off right from the start. She'd make no bones about it. He could pursue her all he wanted. . . . She wouldn't be caught.

Bending her head, she concentrated hard on her breakfast. She could hear her blood roaring in panic even above the raucous laughter of the boaters. What she couldn't hear were Cutter's footsteps as he approached her table.

"Good morning," he greeted her cheerfully. "If the weather here is one of your responsibilities, you've done a great job. Looks like it's going to be another beautiful day."

Sabrina's head snapped up, and her eyes flew to Cutter's face. "You'll be able to enjoy it more over at one of those tables near the edge of the patio, where the sun's shining in under the canopy," she pointed out tightly. Brazen, she thought inwardly. Only a man like Cutter would walk right up to her table when she was obviously trying to ignore him.

"I take it then that you don't fraternize with your guests?" Cutter asked. One of his hands rested on the back of the chair next to hers. It looked work roughened and strong and incredibly masculine. The sea and salty air had taken their toll on his skin. His touch would be rough. But practiced, too, she thought. He'd be able to use those weather-worn hands to elicit a thunderous response in a woman.

Sabrina shook her head to dash the thoughts away and looked up at him again with a confused frown. "Why do you say that?"

Cutter's smile widened. She was sure her discomfiture pleased him. "Because you've just directed me to a table quite removed from your own."

"You might consider politely taking a hint," she muttered.

"I have no respect for hints. Protocol, yes, but not hints. You didn't answer my question."

"Look, Cutter," she snapped, feeling her temper tug

away from her, "this isn't the Waldorf Astoria. Of course I fraternize with my guests on occasion. I—" She broke off suddenly, her eyes flying to the silvery laughter in his as he lowered himself into the seat beside her. "What do you think you're doing?" she demanded.

"Sitting down. I find it aids digestion," he responded smoothly, reaching past her for a menu.

"Well, you don't aid mine, and what's more, I don't remember inviting you to join me."

"No, I don't suppose you did. But you didn't ask me not to, either, and in a case like this, you have to look for whatever loopholes you can. If I had waited for an outright invitation, I'd be eating breakfast over at that other table." His eyes turned dismissively back to his menu as though his explanation were sufficient reason to end the discussion.

Sabrina panicked. Putting him off was not going to be even remotely as easy as she had thought it would. "That's your problem, Cutter," she snapped. "You grab too many loopholes. Don't you have any respect for other people's wishes?"

His gunmetal eyes came back to her. There wasn't much humor in them now. At the sight of them, cold fingers of alarm began to tickle her spine. The quiet, serious tone of his voice didn't reassure her, either.

"Generally, yes, I do," he answered. "But not always. Not when I want something. Then I can be prone to do just about anything to get it."

"Up to and including being rude?" Her heart fluttered at the implications of his words, but she struggled not to let her reaction show.

"Up to and including eating the mediocre food these

little islands insist upon serving," he mused absently, his eyes scanning the menu again.

For a moment Sabrina was dumbfounded by his response. His audacity, she thought, knew no bounds. Then her voice returned to her, and she ground out, "No one invited you to eat it. No one invited you to Thunder Cay and—"

"It's not a private, invitation-only club, is it?" he cut her off, still not looking up at her.

"Damn you! If you don't like little islands, then why the hell did you come here? You could have stopped at Paradise Island; you could have kept going until you hit Florida—"

"I could have, but I didn't want to," he said, interrupting her again.

"Why?" she demanded incredulously.

"I wanted to stop here. You're here."

Her stomach constricted. His persistence was amazing . . . and frightening.

"I believe that's how this whole conversation got started," he went on mildly. "You were asking me what I'd do to get what I want." He put the menu back on the table and smiled at her devilishly. "I wanted to meet you, so I'm willing to eat mundane food for a while to do it."

Sabrina forced herself to raise her eyebrows at him jauntily. It was all she could do to maintain some semblance of aloof composure. "You can't seriously expect me to believe that you came to Thunder Cay just to meet me," she responded disparagingly. She didn't want to believe it. Premeditation made him seem even more dangerous.

Cutter shrugged. "It's close enough to the truth. I'm

wrapping up the cruise and heading back to Fort Lauderdale. I couldn't see any reason for running hard all the way back when I could stop here for a while and satisfy my curiosity about you."

Sabrina stared at him disbelievingly. She fought off a small shiver and leaned back in her chair again. "Well, now that you've satisfied your curiosity," she answered in her best bored voice, "and since the food we serve is so bad, you might as well just push on. Don't you have some pretty little piece of fluff waiting anxiously for you in Fort Lauderdale?"

Cutter laughed. "Probably, but I find the company much more interesting here. You're fascinating, you know. I haven't even begun to satisfy my curiosity about you. Besides, this was more or less a business cruise, and my business isn't done yet. As long as I'm here trying to get to know the renowned mystery lady of Thunder Cay, I might as well take a look around the island."

Sabrina drew in her breath, but before she could demand to know why he would want to look around her island, he continued. "Besides which, I never said that the food was horrible. Just mediocre and dull. It's not exactly the kind of fare one might expect to find in the finer restaurants of Houston."

Sabrina stiffened. All thoughts of what interest her island might hold for him crumbled as though he had literally smashed them with one of his weather-worn fists. Was he playing games with her? How much did he really know about her? The mention of restaurants and Houston in the same breath seemed too coincidental. Could he somehow know that she had once been married to one of the biggest restaurant entrepreneurs in that city?

After cutting off a piece of ham with a savage little slash of her knife, she popped it into her mouth before answering. She swallowed, then asked carefully, "And what do you know about Houston? The transom of your yacht says you're from Fort Lauderdale."

"Do you believe everything you read?"

Her eyes narrowed as she began to understand. "Are you trying to tell me you're from Houston?"

"Born and raised," Cutter admitted. He turned to give his order to the waiter, who had been hovering near their table. Sabrina hadn't even seen him. She realized disgustedly that the entire building could have burned down around them and she wouldn't have noticed. She was too busy fencing with Cutter.

Ironic, she thought. There was little she hated more than fencing with massive male egos, defending herself against hearsay. She thought she'd left all that behind in Texas . . . but it appeared that Texas had followed her here.

"The *Amazing Grace* is registered in Florida, and I keep a condominium there, but Houston is my home base," Cutter went on, distracting her from her thoughts.

She pushed her plate away abruptly. "And you're an expert on its restaurants," she finished for him tightly. "You don't have a hundred little houseguests fluttering around your kitchen while you cook for them?"

Cutter flashed another grin at her. "Not all at once." At her expression of disbelief, he went on. "What's the matter? Don't you believe I can cook? Or is it that you don't believe I cater to my houseguests?"

"Oh, I'll bet you cater to them, all right," she muttered without thinking.

Cutter's answering chuckle was low and appreciative. "Well, then, it must be my culinary talents that you doubt."

Sabrina cast him a wary look. She was learning to follow his trains of thought. The next thing she knew, he'd be insisting on proving those talents to her.

"I don't think there's much of anything you can't do," she answered quickly. "It's just that I've lived in Houston and, all things considered, I'll bypass its restaurants in favor of the food here."

She had blurted out the first thing that came to her mind. Immediately she regretted it. Cutter was quick to push the issue. "Because you don't like the restaurants or because you don't like the city?" he asked. "Is that where you lived before you decided to seclude yourself here?"

"I don't like living in *any* city," she answered shortly. She hated both Houston and its restaurants, but a man like Cutter could never be expected to understand why.

"Were there many?"

"Many what?" she asked, startled. She had been thinking about Ken and the myriad restaurants and women that had been more important to him than she was. Again she wondered how much Cutter really knew about her.

"Have you lived in many cities?" he said patiently. He leaned back in his chair to allow the waiter to deposit his breakfast in front of him.

Sabrina let out a small sound of relief as she understood his question. "A few," she answered. "Denver, San Diego, L.A. We did a stint in Tacoma once. It was mostly while I was a kid. My family was like a traveling circus. My father never wanted to stay in one place very long. We spent the first twelve years of my life moving from city to city so Dad wouldn't have to grow up and settle down."

"You sound bitter."

Sabrina smiled tightly as she played with her coffee cup. "I always felt like excess baggage," she explained. "Dad would get the itch to move on, and he would leave. Mom would decide that she couldn't live without him, pack me up and follow him. Once, when I overheard them talking about how Dad wanted to leave San Diego, I revolted. I ran away. I used to love the zoo there; it was a place where nothing seemed to change except the addition of new babies once in a while. So I went there. I spent two days sleeping on the benches and hiding from the guards before Mom and Dad put two and two together and descended on me with what seemed like a hundred cops. You know, I honestly didn't believe they would come after me. I figured they would just be glad to get free of me so they could traipse around the country unfettered. I didn't *want* them to come after me." She paused, smiling sadly and distantly. "Those two days I spent at the zoo were some of the happiest I can remember."

"It doesn't sound as though you had the greatest childhood. Or adulthood either, for that matter." Cutter didn't sound entirely sympathetic. There was a gleam of something alert and deductive in his eyes. "How old are you?" he asked suddenly. "Twenty-eight? Twenty-nine?"

"Thirty," she supplied cautiously. What was he getting at?

"And in thirty years, the best time of your life was when you were a kid and ran away?"

She didn't answer him. She didn't dare. He was up to

something, but she couldn't be sure what, so she couldn't plan a counterattack.

"So escaping into a fantasy world helped you once," he went on. "Did you think it would be worth another try twenty years later?"

Sabrina froze. So that was his angle. She realized too late that she had told him much more than she had intended to—much more than she had told anyone since she had been on Thunder Cay, for that matter. And he was using the information to launch into his same old criticisms of her. She glared at him and pointedly turned the subject back to him without answering.

"What about you?" she asked. "Have you always lived in Houston or Florida?"

Cutter eyed her intently for a moment, then obviously decided not to push a subject that was clearly a sore spot with her. For the time being, anyway, she thought sourly.

"I've had an address in Houston since the day I was born," he answered. "It's home. I may spend six months a year down here and in Florida, but I'm always ready to go home to Texas. I usually spend summers there."

Sabrina relaxed imperceptibly as she realized that the conversation had been successfully steered away from her. She rested her chin on her hand, not even realizing that she was smiling at him encouragingly. "How do you manage to spend so much time on the *Amazing Grace?*" she asked. "Don't you work?"

Cutter looked at her disconcertedly for a moment, realizing for the first time how rarely she smiled. My God, what a difference it made in her face! he thought. He had taken for granted that hers was a haunted, ethereal beauty, but now she looked somehow younger and innocent. For the first time since he had met her, her onyx eyes sparkled with the light of the sun and some inner glow. There was more to this woman than even the rumors about her had indicated, he thought. He was uncharacteristically flustered by the discovery.

He had to force himself to cock an eyebrow at her and regain the typically sardonic drawl that was his trademark. "What's this?" he teased. "An expression of interest?"

Sabrina straightened immediately. She dropped her hands back into her lap abruptly. Her smile vanished, and her look became as wry as his had been. Cutter could have kicked himself.

"Hardly," she replied. "I was just trying to establish how much of the reputed playboy you really are. Obviously there's a good-sized chunk in you if you don't work for a living and can afford to spend your winters in the Bahamas."

"Not in the way you define 'playboy.' I work hard so that I can afford to take winters off."

"At what? Making your way into women's beds?"

"That doesn't require work." He laughed as she gaped at him in frustration. "If you don't want to get shot, you shouldn't try dueling with me," he pointed out.

Sabrina stared at him in grim silence.

"That's better. I can't answer your questions while you're throwing verbal darts at me and being catty. I can afford to spend my winters down here because I've finally got my business to the point where it can virtually run itself while I'm gone. I've got a construction company back in Houston."

Sabrina leaned back in her chair and gave him a long, assessing look. "Somehow I can't picture you on your hands and knees hammering nails. Doesn't that clash with your image somewhat? Or do you only play Don Juan in the islands?"

He pushed his plate away and leaned back in his chair again to pull a cigarette from his shirt pocket. "You're being catty again. You've also been listening to rumors again."

"Reputation," she corrected him smugly. "Not rumors. And I'm not being catty. I'm just asking honest, natural questions."

"You're incredible," he murmured. His eyes sought and found hers over his cigarette as he lit it. In the second before the flame of his lighter touched it, neither of them moved. Sabrina felt another thrill of panic dance through her. Old memories were blown through her again like dry autumn leaves on a seductive breeze.

He wanted her. She wasn't going to be able to hold him back. She knew that in a flash. And it was all because of the way she looked and a reputation that he kept insisting she had.

It took everything she had to lean forward calmly and drop her voice to a deliberately sensual whisper. "I'm incredible? Why? Because I'm not falling into your arms?" she asked. "I'll give you some advice on that score, Cutter. Don't hold your breath." She grinned and sat up straight again. "I don't like playboys."

"Ah, but I *do* like challenges."

"Challenges are one thing, but impossibilities are horses of an entirely different color." When he only grinned back at her in his knowing, self-assured way, Sabrina pushed her chair back abruptly. "It's been fun fencing with you, Cutter, but I have work to do."

"No one can work as much as you try to. You're always running off to accomplish something."

"Unfortunately, my marina doesn't run itself the way your construction company seems to. Don't you have to get back to Houston and hammer something?"

"Nope. I haven't actually hammered anything in years. I leave that to the guys I'm paying. I do the brain work. I'm in charge of developments and designing. Things like resorts, hospitals, schools. I create them. The other guys hammer them into place."

Sabrina was halfway to her feet when a warning bell began to sound distantly in the back of her brain. She sat down again slowly. "You enjoy playing games with me, don't you?"

"I enjoy your reactions," he answered honestly. "You've got the most expressive eyes of anyone I've ever met. Sad, but expressive."

She ignored his last gibe and narrowed her eyes at him dangerously. "Really? What are they telling you now?"

"That you're dying to know if my penchant for developing resorts has anything to do with the fact that I want to look over Thunder Cay."

Sabrina felt her heart skip a beat. Its movement made her feel oddly breathless. Even hearing him speak of such a possibility shook her down to her toes.

But she had to know. Straightening her shoulders against the back of her chair, she met his eyes. "Does it?" she asked flatly.

Cutter's eyes began to look more like steel than silver. They were the eyes of a panther waiting patiently for the right time to pounce on his prey. A tiny smile played at the corners of his mouth. "Yes," he answered eventually.

Sabrina sprang to her feet again. She made no pretense of appearing calm now. "Then leave. Now. You can forget the whole idea, because I own four-fifths of the island and I can assure you that I'm not going to sell out to you. I wouldn't consider selling to anyone, much less to someone who would turn this beautiful place into some kind of hedonistic playpen."

Amazingly, Cutter's smile never wavered. Only his eyes grew a shade darker and more serious. "That wasn't my idea. You're believing all those nasty rumors again. I'm not half as shallow and hedonistic as you make me out to be."

It was as though his eyes held some strange power over her. They flickered from her to her chair, and Sabrina felt herself sinking slowly down into it again, as though he had commanded her to. "From what I've learned about you so far, I think you'd be hard pressed to prove it," she managed. Her voice was weak, almost a whisper.

"You haven't given me a chance to prove it." It was amazing, she thought, how he could sound so blasé and look so seductively cunning. It was as though he were circling her, closing in on her, sealing off her avenues of escape . . . with nothing more than words and some carefully cultivated looks. He was just waiting for her to succumb to him.

He'd wait forever.

She forced herself to shrug indifferently. "Has it occurred to you that I don't want to?"

"Many times. But I'm going to change your mind."

He spoke with such quiet certainty that a shiver coursed up Sabrina's spine, one that seemed to come out of nowhere. She felt flushed and hot as she held his eyes. "I wouldn't bet your yacht on it if I were you," she managed. "Not if you cherish it as much as I think you do."

Cutter grinned unperturbedly. "Such a little tiger, aren't you? But you're not half as unyielding and closed-minded as you'd have me believe. Come on, Tiger Eyes. The least you can do is spend a little time with me before you form ironclad opinions and dismiss me and my proposal. Put your work away for a day and come snorkeling with me. I'll tell you all about what I want to do with Thunder Cay."

He wasn't going to let up. He was going to push her until he got what he wanted. She saw all that in the steely determination in his eyes. Chase Cutter wasn't a man to be refused.

The thought made her almost ill with panic before she squared her shoulders determinedly against the back of her chair. Cutter might not be a man to be refused, but *she* wasn't a woman to be bulldozed. Not anymore. She'd allowed herself to be persuaded by a man like him once, and it had been the biggest mistake of her life. She hadn't moved thousands of miles just to get tangled up with another man like her ex-husband—in business or otherwise.

"No," she answered, her voice decisive again. "I can't."

"Why not?"

Her determination waned. Fresh panic fluttered through her. "Would you please give up?" she pleaded. "I've told you I can't. That's all there is to it. I've got too much to do today to take time off. Besides, I'm not at all interested in your proposals."

Cutter's expression turned shrewd. "Aren't you? Or

are you just hell-bent on avoiding me because you're afraid of me?"

Sabrina sucked her breath in sharply. She had never felt so much like a cornered animal in her life. Although he was still leaning back in his chair, she felt as though he were drawing in on her somehow, getting closer. His eyes told her that he had no doubt he would have his way.

She cleared her throat. "Don't be an idiot, Cutter," she answered in the hardest voice she could muster. "Why should I be afraid of you? Unless you're planning to kidnap me and take me against my will? Or maybe you think you can steal away with my island without my knowing it? Forget it, Cutter. You're up against a brick wall this time. It's incredibly difficult to slip off with an island, and the only way you'd get me is by rape."

Cutter's mouth crooked upward in a small smile. "Methinks the lady doth protest too much," he murmured.

"Methinks you don't know when to call it a day. Take my advice, Cutter, and quit now. You can't have Thunder Cay." She paused, then added, "And you can't have me."

Amazingly, Cutter's smile widened until it was almost taunting. "Now we're getting to the crux of the matter. You're not too busy to take the day off, Tiger Eyes. And if this were just a simple matter of discussing a business proposal, you could handle that just fine. No, it's more than that. You and I both know that I'm interested in more than your island. My guess is that that scares the hell out of you. You've forgotten the fine art of flirtation since you've been hibernating here, and you're petrified to give it another try while you're so rusty."

41

A faint trembling started deep inside Sabrina. It was more than just the thrill of panic that had claimed her as he'd circled in for the kill. It was the desperate throb of fear that came from knowing she was virtually caught. He was stringing words around her, snaring her, sealing her fate with silver eyes that were somehow able to see inside her.

She forced herself to shrug, and swallowed hard. "Fine," she answered flippantly. "I've forgotten the fine art of flirtation. But I've done it because I wanted to. It's not worth remembering—and certainly not with you. You're wasting valuable time here, Cutter. You should be off looking for another island for your resort. Not to mention the fact that if you're going to have a fling on this island, you'd best start looking for someone more receptive to your brand of charm. I'm not your type."

She slid out of her chair and got to her feet again as she finished. She wouldn't—*couldn't*—give him a chance to spring another titillating little line on her, something that would make her sit down again and give herself up like a calf for slaughter.

But like the panther she couldn't help likening him to, Cutter rose from his chair as well with swift, sleek intent. He was standing in front of her, blocking her way, before she could even take a step to escape.

"I don't have a type, Tiger Eyes. I'm open to suggestions," he murmured.

He stood so close to her. If she moved as much as an inch she would touch him. Crazily, she thought she could feel the heat of him. She had to struggle to find her voice again.

"Then let me make one," she countered eventually,

her voice breathless. "Go find someone who will believe your polished lines, and practice your flirtation on her."

"I don't believe in wasted energy. Why should I look for someone else when I've found you?"

"Won't work. I've forgotten the fine art of flirtation, remember?"

She realized belatedly that it was the worst thing she could possibly have said to him. It was like waving a red blanket in front of a bull. Cutter latched on to her retort immediately. His slow answering smile told her more clearly than words that she had been caught. Tension and fear burned through her.

"No you haven't," Cutter answered. "No, not really. You're just badly in need of a refresher course."

Sabrina's heart hurtled into her throat as she met his eyes. He was serious. He wasn't just playing games with her now, trying to tease a reaction out of her. She saw something in his gaze that no woman could fail to recognize. He wanted her in the most elemental sense. And he wasn't the type to be denied.

She swallowed hard. "Maybe, but you're not going to be the one to give it to me." As she finished, she tried to step around him.

Cutter's reflex was like lightning. He reached out and snagged her arm. It wasn't an uncompromising grip she couldn't have broken, yet Sabrina went still. Her heart thundered as her eyes came slowly back to him, watching, waiting.

He was through stalking her. The end was near. She could feel it in the air, could see it in his eyes.

"That's where you're wrong," he answered, his voice husky. "I think I qualify for the job perfectly. I'm willing to take my time. I'll be here for a while. You need someone who's willing to devote some energy to you, someone you can't dismiss after one night with those forbidding tiger eyes."

"Which is precisely why I don't need you. I'm dismissing you, Cutter." It was a futile effort and she knew it, but she tried to pull away from him.

Cutter's grip still didn't tighten. He caught her instead with his mouth, bringing it down on hers. Sabrina gasped, and her eyes flew open wide as he turned her slightly to face him without once lifting his lips. It was a smooth, expert move, she thought, and then she was no longer able to consider the amount of practice that had undoubtedly gone into it.

Cutter hadn't closed his eyes, either. For a brief second they held hers, so close that she could see flecks of black in them now. They transfixed her with their sooty intensity, immobilizing her, and in that scant second, understanding flashed in on her with even more clarity than it had before. He wanted her. He intended to have her. And even if she managed to pull away from him now, he'd be back.

Panic screamed just beneath her skin.

He pulled her closer, uncaring of the eyes all around them. Sabrina brought her hands to his chest instinctively, intending to push him away. But her splayed fingers found hard, firm muscles beneath the fabric of his shirt, and she forgot what she had meant to do, forgot that he was a threat to her carefully shuttered world. A tiny spot of warmth began to grow inside her.

It mingled with her blood as it expanded, rushing through her. She felt light-headed and weak and as though her skin were on fire. The sensations rocketed through her, frightening her. They were stronger than she was.

Without realizing she was doing it, she ran her hands up his chest to his shoulders, savoring the subdued strength with which he held her. Her eyes fluttered closed. Her mouth yielded to his.

His tongue traced the fullness of her mouth; then his lips covered hers completely. His mouth was hard, his tongue searching as it dipped past hers. His hold on her tightened fractionally as he felt her soften against him. For a split second his kiss became even more demanding, as though to force even more of a response from her. Then, before she could even react to the demand, his arms fell away from her. She could feel the electricity of decision as it filtered through him, making his muscles even more rigid and tense.

True to his word, he was going to take his time with her.

Sabrina stepped backward quickly as he released her. She more than expected to find his smile mocking her again. Instead his expression was serious. She saw controlled hunger in his eyes.

"No, you're not so unyielding, Tiger Eyes," he said in a silky voice. "And you don't have so much to learn. I think you'll need only a very short refresher course before we can get down to basics."

"Basics?" she croaked. "Oh, my God. You're crazy."

Cutter's only response was a satisfied smile as he leaned down and signed the tab the waiter had left on the table. His grin widened as he straightened and met her eyes again. Then he turned and walked away without saying anything more. But Sabrina knew he wasn't really going anywhere, that he wouldn't wander far. He'd be back.

She sat down hard in her chair again. She felt a thrill of fear wash through her as she realized there was every chance that she could lose this battle Chase Cutter was waging with her. And everything men had ever taught her told her that the price of losing would be dear.

3

And if Sabrina would join us long enough to take part in the discussion, we might be able to decide what to do about it."

Sabrina's eyes snapped away from the open doorway to the bar and settled fretfully on the statuesque black woman who sat across the table from her. Scowling, she pushed her dinner plate away. Her meal was virtually untouched. She had spent the last hour watching the door, waiting for Cutter to arrive. She had no doubt that he would.

"What to do about what?" she asked Taura Lyons, her general manager.

"Getting a helicopter. We almost *have* to find room in the budget for it, Sabrina," she answered. "The population on the island is growing. We've had four medical emergencies this year alone, not counting Mary Lou deciding to have her baby this morning. We need something faster than a boat to get us to Nassau or the mainland."

Dwight, the office manager, spoke up. "It would step up mail delivery, too."

Sabrina looked from one to the other vacantly. She felt like a fool, but she simply hadn't been paying attention to the conversation. "Mary Lou had her baby *this morning?*" she asked. The girl worked behind the counter in the commissary. Her baby hadn't been due for another month yet.

Taura grinned. "She had a seven-pound boy. Pretty hefty for coming a month early." Then her smile faded. "The point is that Mary Lou was supposed to take the boat over to Nassau at the end of the month and stay with her aunt until the baby came—for the express purpose of avoiding what happened this morning. She barely made it to the hospital, Sabrina. She came damned close to having the baby on the boat because it took so long to get her to Nassau. We've got to come up with a better means of transportation. We can't keep risking the islanders' health like this. They depend on us."

Sabrina nodded dully. The fact of the matter was that there was no room in the budget for something as extravagant as a helicopter. She had opened her mouth to remind Taura of that when she realized that the other woman wasn't looking at her.

Cold fingers trekked up Sabrina's spine as she twisted slightly in her chair to follow Taura's gaze. But despite their icy caress, she felt something hot coast through her when she saw what had snagged Taura's attention.

Cutter was making his way into the restaurant. His arm was draped casually over Marci's shoulders.

"She's, uh . . ." Sabrina began, then paused to clear her throat. "She's supposed to be the wife of the other guy on board," she told Taura inanely.

Taura's gaze swiveled back to her. She shrugged. "Could be. I've heard that Chase Cutter has no respect for matrimony."

Sabrina nodded distractedly. No, he wouldn't, she thought, no matter what he had told her about his views on married women. Men like Cutter had very little respect for anything—and most certainly not other men's wives.

She turned back to Taura abruptly. "About this situation with Mary Lou," she began, changing the subject more harshly and quickly than was necessary. "I take it that she *did* get to the hospital all right, even though it was close? Where the hell was I when all this was going on? We *do* have shuttle planes coming in and out of here once in a while. Maybe there was one in the area and we could have caught him on the radio, gotten him to make an emergency stop. Why wasn't I consulted?"

"Because you were kissing Chase Cutter," Taura responded bluntly. "And I thought it was prudent not to interrupt you."

Sabrina recoiled visibly at the other woman's words. Of course it was too much to hope that no one had noticed that little fiasco. But she *had* prayed that no one would have the nerve to mention it. She ran a hand over her forehead, paling considerably. What a fool she had been to think that such a juicy occurrence wouldn't become grist for the local gossip mill! Damn Cutter!

"It would be also be prudent not to mention it again," she warned Taura tightly.

Dwight's eyes darted from one woman to the other as

the tension at the table escalated. In an effort to restore peace he leaned forward and joked, "Look at it this way, Sabrina. If it gets out that you two are having a fling, business will boom and we'll get the new helicopter. People will come in droves to find out what Cutter's up to now. Not to mention the fact that you pique quite a bit of local interest yourself. Talk about advertising!"

She turned on him in barely controlled fury. "We are *not* having a fling, nor are we going to. My reputation will *not* be used as an advertisement for Thunder Cay!" She paused and took a deep breath, remembering the way Ken had used her to promote business. The memory made her shake. Leave it to Cutter to open those old wounds all over again, she thought viciously.

She turned back to the stunned faces of Taura and Dwight, realizing belatedly that the three of them had always shared a jovial, easygoing relationship. They wouldn't understand her burst of temper.

"Sorry," she muttered. "You hit a sore spot. Just do me a favor and try to keep a lid on any rumors that might pop up about Cutter and me. They're not true."

Dwight and Taura exchanged looks. "Sure thing," Taura murmured, then quickly changed the subject. "The accountant's coming in next Friday. Why don't we sit down with him then and figure out the feasibility of this helicopter idea?"

Sabrina nodded slowly. Adrenaline was draining out of her, leaving her with an empty feeling. "Sounds good to me," she answered quietly.

"Good. That's a start, anyway." Taura turned to Dwight. "Care to join me in the bar for a nightcap?"

Sabrina watched distractedly as the two made their way into the bar. Then her eyes moved restlessly to

Cutter's table again. His head was bent close to Marci's. As she watched, the two drew apart and laughed.

Sabrina felt her stomach tighten painfully. How dare he come to her island to flaunt his sexual prowess! she thought scathingly. For that matter, how dare he put her in the line of fire in full view of everyone who worked for her? It was bad enough that he had set tongues to wagging by kissing her right on the damned patio! Now he was churning things up even more by expanding his horizons with Marci.

Before she realized what she was doing, she was on her feet. Three long, purposeful strides carried her to Cutter's table.

His silver eyes roamed upward to meet hers. They took their time along the way, sliding over the curve of her hips beneath the tight denim skirt she wore, then over the fullness of her breasts beneath her sheer cotton blouse. Almost insolently they hovered at her open neckline, studying the darkly tanned skin at her throat. Sabrina felt her pulse twitch there, then start to flutter. Heat seemed to consume her. She could feel it coloring her cheeks.

What have I done? Her thoughts screamed at her in confusion and embarrassment. Cutter's gaze held hers as he waited for her to say something.

She cleared her throat awkwardly. "I take it you didn't have much luck snorkeling today?" she asked inanely, searching for something safely neutral to say. Her temper was already fizzling out.

Cutter raised an eyebrow at her. "On the contrary. We caught all sorts of things." There was a confirming laugh from Marci. Cutter's gaze flicked to her briefly, then came back to Sabrina again. "Four lobsters," he supplied.

"Not to mention a fantastic array of shells, one tiny grouper and a very large case of sunburn."

Sabrina couldn't help herself. She threw a quick glance at Marci, then another one back to Cutter. They were both brown as berries. No sunburn there.

Cutter followed her gaze, then laughed aloud. "John— Marci's husband—has the sunburn. Which is why he couldn't join us tonight. We left him back on the yacht to lick his wounds."

"Or slather moisturizer all over himself, as the case may be," Marci contributed. "We shouldn't really be laughing at his expense, I suppose," she added, sighing but not looking at all contrite. "He *is* suffering."

"Not as much as I am," Cutter muttered. His eyes stayed on Sabrina's. They challenged her to respond.

"You? Suffering?" she asked with a sardonic grin. "What an interesting concept."

"Ah, but I am. I could have been eating lobster tonight."

"As opposed to my restaurant's mundane fare?"

Cutter's grin widened. "I'm into sacrificing these days," he reminded her. "It has its merits. I had it on good authority that you usually eat here with your managers."

Sabrina bristled again. "And who supplied you with that information?"

Cutter gave her a wry look. "One of those rumormongers we were talking about."

Sabrina stared at him grimly. "People talk entirely too much around here."

"Can you blame them? Outside of the occasional unexpected birth, there's really not much to keep them occupied. Calm down, Tiger Eyes. I would have eaten here anyway. I'm saving my share of the lobster."

Sabrina opened her mouth to ask him how he knew about Mary Lou, then realized it was a moot point anyway. He was right. People talked on Thunder Cay—a lot. Instead she asked, "Until you can find an enterprising female to eat it with you?"

"Until I can convince her to have dinner with me, yes."

She should have known that he wouldn't mince words. Still, her heart somersaulted at the confidence in his tone, and she glanced around quickly to see if anyone had overheard him. As she turned back to him, a memory of his kiss flashed through her mind. For a breathless moment she remembered the way her senses had spun when he had touched her, and the strange warmth that had suffused her.

But a kaleidoscope of other memories was hiding behind that one: Dwight's joking speculation, Cutter's head bent close to Marci's . . . and older ones that she had thought she'd left behind forever. She backed away from the table as though she had suddenly discovered a snake sitting on top of it.

"You'd better start looking for her, then," she responded tightly. "Lobster is best served fresh." She gave him a short nod and turned away from the table.

Cutter's mocking voice stopped her. "Running off to work again?" he asked. "Or just from another challenge?"

Sabrina whirled around to face him, then swallowed hard. She would not let him make her lose her cool. "I'm going back to work," she answered coolly. "Call it public relations. I like to mingle with my guests on occasion."

"You're doing that now," Cutter pointed out.

"I think I'm needed more elsewhere. You seemed to be entertaining yourself quite well before I came along."

She didn't give him a chance to respond but turned away again quickly. A desperate fluttering inside her tried to goad her into hurrying, but she refused to give Cutter the satisfaction. Forcing her steps into a sedate rhythm, she made her way into the bar.

Dwight and Taura were at a table near the back, and she decided not to disturb them. Instead she slid onto a stool at the far end of the bar and surveyed the room unseeingly.

She accepted a drink from the bartender and swallowed gratefully. It seemed as if only seconds had passed before the barstool next to hers scraped back against the floor. Sabrina snapped her head up and twisted around to meet Cutter's probing silver eyes again.

"So this is how Tiger Eyes spends her evenings," he murmured, sliding onto the stool. He ordered a drink, then turned back to her again. "I'd wondered," he went on enigmatically.

"Wondered what?" Sabrina asked irritably, staring down into her glass. She didn't dare look at him. She knew what his gaze could do to her. It froze her, trapped her. It made her lose herself.

"What happens to you when the sun goes down," Cutter went on equably. "Rumor has it that you fade into the shadows of the night, never to be seen again until dawn."

"Damn it, Cutter! Will you knock it off with these rumors people are supposed to be telling about me?" she snapped, finally looking up at him. She knew immediately that he had just been fishing for a reaction again. His eyes laughed back at her.

"Perhaps I should," he answered. "They're obviously wrong. In that respect, anyway. The sun has gone down and you haven't faded. In fact, you're as beautiful and as impossible to ignore as ever." He took a sip of his drink and flashed a grin at her. "So tell me, do you spend all your nights like this?"

"For the most part," she answered tightly.

"For the most part," Cutter echoed in a speculative voice. "But not the whole part. What else do you do?"

Sabrina stiffened defensively. "What are you getting at? What difference does it make?"

"You intrigue me. I've made no bones about it, have I? I want to know what you do, how you live, whatever."

Sabrina stared at him, her eyes wide and dark. Fresh alarm curled through her like deadly smoke. He could deceive her so easily if she let him, she thought. He could almost make her believe that he cared about something other than her looks and his ego.

"Are you going to answer me?" he prodded her eventually. His gaze continued to hold hers steadily.

"I've forgotten the question," she muttered uncomfortably.

"What else do you do when the sun goes down?" he persisted.

"Probably something quite different from what you do."

"We won't know unless we compare notes."

Sabrina cast him an exasperated look out of the corner of her eye. "I have a business to run, although you have a convenient way of forgetting that. The marina is a twenty-four-hour operation. Sometimes things call for my attention in the evenings. When they do, I work."

Cutter's gaze turned speculative. "It follows, then, that you either work at night or sit here in the bar watching your customers," he mused. Then his disarming grin was back, and she knew he was just moving in for the kill. "Sounds horribly boring to me."

"No one asked for your opinion."

"I've volunteered a lot more than you've asked for," he pointed out. His voice was just a shade softer than before, intimating a vague sense of intimacy. Sabrina could not have doubted what he meant.

"You didn't protest then," he went on.

It wasn't something she wanted to be reminded of. She could still see that kiss happening in her mind's eye . . . the way he had turned her toward him without lifting his mouth from hers, such a polished move and so suave. The way she had lifted her hands to push him away and ended up doing nothing more than caressing the firm, hard muscles of his chest, shocking herself, becoming a stranger to herself.

"I'll take boring over meaningless seduction anytime," she snapped.

Cutter raised an eyebrow at her. "Kissing you was meaningless seduction? Is that what you think?" His voice was almost too casual.

Sabrina glared at him. Why was he backing her into a corner like this? They both knew what he wanted from her; they both knew that his desire for her was as shallow as a summer day is long.

"I think you're a master of meaningless seduction," she began carefully, then blurted, "Oh, come on, Cutter.

I'm not blind. I saw you out there in the restaurant with Marci less than twelve hours after you grabbed and kissed me!''

Amazingly, he laughed. Sabrina sucked in her breath in anger as he taunted, "Is the lady jealous?"

She drew herself up, squaring her shoulders as she met his eyes. "You've got to be kidding," she scoffed.

"Just asking," Cutter chuckled.

"Then permit me to answer you. Jealousy would imply that I want to be in Marci's shoes. I can assure you that I don't." She turned back to her drink, only to realize that the glass was empty. She caught the bartender's eye and pointed to her glass irritably.

"Well, then," Cutter murmured, "if you're not jealous of Marci, you must be jealous of me."

"Jealous of *you?*" Sabrina was so astounded that she gaped at him. "Cutter, your ego is amazing! Why on earth would I be jealous of you?"

"Because I was enjoying myself. Maybe you envied me because you weren't."

So they were back to that again. Sabrina tossed back some of her drink and glared at him. Why was it that she was always defending her lifestyle to him?

"Spare me," she responded cuttingly. "I think I've already mentioned—on numerous occasions—that I have the quiet, uncomplicated life I've always wanted. Believe me when I tell you that I'm not jealous of anyone."

"Quiet and uncomplicated is one thing," he answered. "Hibernation is another." There was a serious, almost annoyed tone in his voice now that was new. Then she remembered his plans for developing the island. Of course he doesn't want me to hibernate here, she thought. He wants the place for himself.

She opened her mouth to say as much, but he cut her off. "I don't know why you're doing it, but I suspect I'll find out eventually," he went on. His eyes were probing her soul again. She stared at him, mesmerized by the silvery intent she saw there.

"Doing what?" she managed to ask.

"Hiding here, for starters."

"For God's sake, Cutter, I'm not—"

He cut her off again. "I'd bet the *Amazing Grace* that you're running away from something in Houston. But you can't run on a permanent basis, Tiger Eyes. You can get away for a month, maybe six, maybe even a couple of years—but not forever. Given enough time, everything will catch up with you."

"I thought you were a carpenter, not a psychiatrist," she bit out. What was it about her life that fascinated him so? Why wouldn't he leave it alone?

"I'm not a psychiatrist," he answered. "But I've taken my lumps and learned my lessons. I've come to recognize someone else who's nursing a lump, so to speak. And you are. You're too young and beautiful to stagnate here on Thunder Cay for the rest of your life, Tiger Eyes. Sooner or later you're going to have to go back to do battle with the real world again." He paused, then added as an afterthought, "No matter how frightened you are."

Sabrina swallowed the remainder of her drink in one gulp and motioned irritably at the bartender for another. In the minutes it took him to deliver it, she forced herself to breathe deeply and evenly. Anger was burgeoning inside her, trying to strangle her.

She sipped at her new drink more slowly, then forced herself to turn back to the man who just would not leave her alone. "Just how naive do you think I am, Cutter? Do you honestly believe I'd take the advice of a stranger who knows nothing about me and run back to Houston and abandon my island? Wait—let me rephrase that. I wouldn't be abandoning it. I'd be delivering it straight into your hands."

Cutter chuckled softly. "I was wondering when you'd get around to mentioning that. I'm not trying to wrangle your island away from you. Relax."

Surprise made her risk another quick look into his eyes. "You've changed your mind? You're not interested in developing Thunder Cay after all?"

"I didn't say that."

Her hope fizzled out almost before it had been able to take root. "You're just playing games with me again, is that it?"

"I'm not doing that, either. It's just that for the moment I was thinking about you. If I was advising you to go back to the real world, it was because I think you could gain a lot by that, not because it would give me the opportunity to snatch up the island."

Sabrina glared at him through eyes that were narrowed with anger. God, men could be so smoothly solicitous when they tried! "You don't know me well enough to know what I'd gain by anything," she responded flatly.

"Not yet," he answered. His smile was confident. "But I will. And in the meantime, I think I know human nature well enough to form an opinion. I'm not against running away from things for a while. Hell, I've done it myself—

everyone has at one point or another. I'm only saying that it can't be done forever. And if I've got an interest in Thunder Cay—or any other island, for that matter—it's based on exactly that premise. People need to run away once in a while. I just want to give them a place to escape to. Temporarily, of course."

She gave him a scathing look. "With a high-rise hotel complex, five pools, plenty of pickup bars and half a dozen airliners running back and forth between the mainland, no doubt."

Cutter raised an eyebrow at her reprovingly. "Not quite. Your figures are off a bit."

"It doesn't matter. You're not going to do it here."

His response was quick and cutting. "You'd rather see your employees having babies on boats?"

Sabrina's eyes snapped back to him. "First of all, your gossipmongers have screwed up again. Mary Lou had her baby in the Nassau hospital. Second, it's none of your business anyway. And third," she ground out, "it has nothing at all to do with your pipe dreams of creating a singles utopia on my island."

"It has everything to do with it," he answered in a gentle voice that infuriated her. "Look, we both know that nothing's sacred around here. People talk, and I've been listening to them. I know that you're just barely making ends meet. The marina's not losing money, but it's not making a whole hell of a lot, either. And you've got quite a few islanders and employees depending on you. So, the way I see it, you've got two choices. You can throw in with me, do the place up right, and give them their helicopters, medical services and whatnot within a year or so. Or you can go along as you have been, and everyone can wait until who knows how many years down the pike when you start making some real money."

"They'll have to wait," Sabrina answered in a choked voice. "I've never cared for taking shortcuts."

"Not even when they get you to the same place?"

"It's not the same place!" she exploded, draining her glass and smacking it down on the bar again. "You're talking about a resort! Thunder Cay's not a resort—it's a little port, a place to rest for a while halfway back to the mainland. If you get your way, I might as well go back to Houston! People would start descending on the island like it was some sort of vacation spot. As far as I'm concerned, if they're looking for glitter and lights, they can go to Nassau."

"And you'll just stay here and hibernate and starve."

"Stop it, Cutter," she warned.

He ignored her. "You're being selfish. There's no reason in the world why you can't share your little utopia, lend a hand to the people who depend on you, and make some money for yourself besides."

She'd had enough. She couldn't listen to this anymore. Her stomach was in a knot. She pushed her stool back and got to her feet. "The discussion's over, Cutter," she announced. "I've got a big day tomorrow. I've got to . . ." She trailed off. Amazingly, the room was moving, turning itself just a bit off-center.

Cutter's bark of laughter brought her bewildered eyes to his. "I wondered if you were going to be able to hold all of that," he chuckled. "What the hell were you drinking? What are those concoctions?" He nodded toward her empty glass.

"Mai tais," she answered weakly, then jumped a bit as

61

Cutter leaned toward her. For a wild, paranoid moment she thought he was going to kiss her again, but he only leaned across the bar and reached for her purse.

"Calm down, Tiger Eyes," he cautioned in an amused voice that told her clearly he hadn't missed a thing. "I'm just going to walk you home. You're right—the discussion's over for the time being. You're rapidly becoming intoxicated."

"No, I'm fine," she protested. "I'm just . . ." She trailed off again uncertainly, her gaze dropping to her hands. Cutter's strong, calloused fingers were gently prying hers apart. His touch, innocent though it was, seemed to create waves in her blood. She felt oddly warm and fluttery as he pushed her purse into her hands.

Then the sensation drained away as he began to steer her toward the door. Outside on the patio, she pulled away from him abruptly. "What do you think you're doing?"

"I'm seeing you home safely." By the time he finished speaking, he was holding her arm again. This time his grip was a bit tighter.

"I think you're confused, Cutter," she snapped, struggling against him. "This isn't Houston. I can get back to my apartment safely under my own steam."

Suddenly his grip tightened even more. He stopped walking, dragging her to a stop with him. Sabrina turned back to him, startled. His eyes looked like diamonds in the scant light filtering out of the bar and restaurant. Hard diamonds, she thought.

"I've let you have your fun with this rumor business, Tiger Eyes," he growled. Something in his voice alerted her to the fact that he was genuinely angry. "But now I'm going to disillusion you on one aspect of it. Whatever else you've heard about me, the truth is that I have a certain code of honor. I wouldn't allow any woman of mine to make her way back home alone after she'd been drinking."

Panic made her voice sarcastic. "That sounds reasonable. But I'm not 'a woman of yours,' so you can let me go."

His hold on her relaxed, but he didn't release her. Even if he had, she knew the gesture wouldn't have done anything to dispel the tension sizzling in the air between them.

"No," he murmured thoughtfully. "I'll agree with you there. You're not just any woman, not like any I've known. You're frustrating and maddening and intriguing."

Sabrina gently pulled away from his loose grip. Slowly, carefully, she backed away from him. "That's only because you can't have me, Cutter," she answered softly, the fight draining out of her. "Men always want what they can't have. And once they get it, they throw it away and move on to the next challenge. I have no intention of giving you the chance to throw me away."

"It's not me you're refusing to give a chance to," he countered. "It's a nonexistent man built of rumors who you've been fighting off. Ridiculous rumors. Stop using them as a weapon against me."

Sabrina laughed hollowly. "Come on, Cutter. One of the things you're not is obtuse. Rumors aren't ridiculous. They're dangerous. Trust me, I know. And too many of them are following you around. I'm not going to get tangled up with them again."

"Again?"

She turned on him, an old, heavy anger clogging her

throat. "That's right. Again. I spent years fighting off rumors that my ex-husband obligingly embellished for me in the interest of his own reputation and business. They were my own personal rumors, and granted, right now we're talking about yours, but it doesn't really make any difference. They're there. I don't like them. I didn't move halfway around the world just to have them haunt me again. What's more, I have no way of knowing that yours aren't true, and I'm not going to take the chance that they are. As I've mentioned before, I don't like playboys."

She turned away from him, but she didn't hurry. She was too tired of fighting him off. She felt as though she had been fighting off men like him for a lifetime.

She had reached the door to her apartment before she became aware of his presence again. As she fumbled with her key, Cutter reached out to take it from her. Before she was entirely sure of what was happening, he had unlocked the door and stepped inside.

Sabrina followed, blinking up at him in the soft light from the desk lamp that she had left on earlier. He looked ominous in the murky near-darkness, so tall, with his broad shoulders silhouetted against the light behind him.

"Cutter." Her voice was a groan. "Don't do this to me. Just leave it be. Go find someone else to stalk."

"Not quite yet, Tiger Eyes. First I'm going to prove to you that you're hiding from something worthwhile. Then, if you still want me to leave you alone, I will."

He reached out for her and drew her into his arms again. Sabrina felt the room tumble away as his mouth claimed hers. Some small part of her reminded her that she didn't want him to hold her, didn't want him to kiss her, but she couldn't find her voice to tell him so, and couldn't find the strength to push him away.

There was a sense of purpose in his kiss, just as there had been before. It was the near-violent intent of a panther who finally has his prey between his paws. When she finally found the will to try to pull away from him, his strong, calloused hand caught the back of her neck and pressed her toward him again. She was aware of his strength, so much greater than hers and barely leashed.

She tried to rationalize her reaction in the small part of her brain that was still functioning. It was useless to fight him, she told herself. He was stronger than she was. He thought he had a point to prove. The most sensible thing to do would be to let him think he'd proved it, then send him on his way.

She had to believe that, because her arms were going around his neck almost of their own accord. Her lips parted as though they, too, had a mind of their own. Besides, whatever else he was, he was excitement. He made her blood crash in waves. He electrified her.

She forgot that she didn't want him to touch her. Something close to desperation raced through her. It told her that she needed him, demanded that she allow herself to feel again.

She moaned when his mouth left hers and found the pulse that had been fluttering at her throat virtually from the minute she had stepped up to his table in the restaurant. She heard herself saying his name, half in weak protest, half in hunger. Her body took on a life of its own, pressing against him without waiting for her mind's permission. She thought she saw a smile touch Cutter's lips as he lifted his head to kiss her again, but then she forgot about it. His fingers found the peak of her breast through the thin cotton of her blouse, eliciting another moan from her.

The sound of her own voice, velvety with passion, seemed to destroy the last of her resistance. Suddenly she *needed* to feel the invasion of his tongue as it sought hers. She *needed* his touch as his hands coasted along the curves of her body. She tried to press still closer to him, seeking the heat of his mouth. The waves in her blood roared and churned as his tongue sought hers with savage determination. Her own passion made her legs feel weak.

When he began to back away from her infinitesimally, she nearly stumbled. His hands found her shoulders and pushed her away from him gently . . . too gently. She stared up at him in confusion, her heart thundering.

"I issue fair warning," he murmured in a throaty voice. "I'm about to violate another one of those rumors you've been clinging to."

Parts of her brain were slowly beginning to activate themselves again. The woman she had always known herself to be began to return to her gradually. She hugged herself, feeling cold. Shock at her own behavior made her voice hard and defensive.

"You don't violate them, Cutter," she muttered. "You play them to the hilt."

His answering grin chilled her. "Wrong again, Tiger Eyes." He released her and moved around her toward the door. "The man you'd like to think I am would be in bed with you in about . . ." He trailed off, glancing down at his watch. "Oh, maybe ten, fifteen minutes. But the man I really am is going to wait until you're sober."

A different kind of heat began to suffuse her. Embarrassment colored her cheeks and choked the air out of her lungs. She moved quickly behind the counter into the kitchen to shield herself in the shadows there.

"I thought you were a man with a point to prove," she snapped. "Why the sudden sense of honor?"

Infuriatingly, he winked at her as he pulled the door open and stepped outside. "I don't always take shortcuts either."

4

‱‱‱‱‱‱‱‱

He hadn't lied to her. Cutter rarely took shortcuts. Toward that end, he drove the dilapidated CJ7 he had borrowed at a rather high cost from one of the islanders through the roughest terrain of the island. He had seen enough of the areas that were already in use. Now he was interested in the rest of the island, untouched land that was ripe for development.

He stopped the Jeep as he reached a copse of trees that wouldn't allow him to go any further. Scowling, he glanced around, trying to get his bearings. He decided that he was at the extreme northern tip of Thunder Cay. It was little more than an isolated spit of land, the center overgrown with tropical brush and trees, the edges forming a white beach that should have been on a postcard. It was beautiful, the perfect place for a retreat. But he wasn't looking for perfect scenery at the moment. He was figuring the logistics and placement of cottages, trying to determine where the land would best support them. Later he would decide which of those probable places offered the best views and start planning.

If he could ever convince Sabrina Caide to kick in with him on the whole idea.

Scowling again, he shifted into reverse and threw his arm over the passenger seat to peer over his shoulder as he backed up. The truth of the matter was that he was much less sure of that possibility now than he had been four days ago.

Ah, but he hadn't met a woman yet who didn't have her price, he thought as he reached a spot wide enough to turn around in. Still, Sabrina Caide seemed . . . well, different. He had no idea what her price might be. And he was actually beginning to wonder if she *did* have one.

He shifted back into first and began to maneuver the Jeep around. It wasn't easy. The road was nothing more than two deep ruts formed in the dirt by years of use. It really was the ideal island for his resort, he thought again.

The thought made him more determined than ever to talk some sense into Sabrina. It was only when he looked up at the beach inadvertently that his thoughts shifted away from possible ways to convince her to sell. Slowly, thoughtfully, he shifted back into neutral and braced his arms against the steering wheel.

"Speak of the devil," he murmured aloud.

Sabrina stood twenty feet into the surf. Naked? He leaned up over the steering wheel to get a better view. If she wasn't, she was nearly so. Waves crashed around her hips, concealing them. Cutter leaned back again, his forehead furrowing in a small frown of concentration. The rigidly controlled woman he had had breakfast with didn't seem the type to swim in the nude. But the woman he had kissed in her apartment? It was possible. His frown deepened. God, she was hard to figure out.

One thing was certainly indisputable, though. She was beautiful. He reached down to turn off the ignition without taking his eyes from her, then settled back in his seat and pulled a cigarette from his shirt pocket. He lit it without looking at it. His gaze never left her.

She stood with her back toward him. Her wet skin gleamed like bronze in the bright sunlight. Her long black hair was twisted forward over her shoulder. As he watched, she raised her arms and dove neatly over an incoming wave. No, she wasn't wearing a swimsuit. Something tightened inside him, an unbelievably strong sense of wanting. It surprised him. He couldn't remember the last time he had denied himself anything. Why was he doing it now?

He wasn't. At least, not entirely, he admitted. She was denying him. She had been avoiding him for days, ever since that night in her apartment. That was something new, too. He wasn't quite sure what to make of it. He might have walked out of her apartment that night of his own volition, but he couldn't deny the doubts that made him wonder if he could have had her even if he had stayed.

Yes, she was different. She was an enigma. He had never come across a woman like her before.

He continued to watch as she surfaced again and swam away from the shore, but now he wasn't really seeing her. His mind's eye was stuck on the image of her diving over that wave, her body looking wet and sleek and brown.

Suddenly he ground out his cigarette in the ashtray

and sprang out of the Jeep. She probably wasn't going to like this, not at all, but he was going to join her. I'm like an alcoholic who needs a drink, he thought sourly, but he was smiling. The truth of the matter was that he couldn't wait to see her eyes flashing at him in anger when she became aware of his presence. That anger presented a very clear challenge to him. He was determined to make it go away.

He stripped off his clothes quickly and started toward the water, expecting her to turn around and spot him at any moment. She didn't. She was floating on her back now, looking utterly relaxed. Her arms were outstretched, her breasts pointed toward the sun. She looked primitive and wild that way, with her hair fanned out around her.

He slipped into the water quietly and dove under the next wave. The water was clear enough to allow him to see her in the distance. Years of snorkeling enabled him to hold his breath long enough to reach her. He surfaced beside her.

Sabrina's pulse skyrocketed in panic as he broke through the water. Surprise made her tense, and she began to sink. Sputtering, she righted herself and turned on him. This was amazing! She had an entire island at her disposal, and yet he seemed to find her again and again! They had been going through this for days—wherever she hid, he'd find her. She had spent four entire days leaving one place or another, trying to avoid him.

Her eyes flashed fire at him, just as he had known they would. "For God's sake, Cutter, this has gone on long enough!"

He grinned at her with a feigned innocence that he

knew would infuriate her further. "What's gone on long enough?" he asked.

"You're stalking me, damn it!" she ground out. "Who do you think you are? I hate to break it to you, Cutter, but this isn't a jungle, and I have no intention of becoming your trophy!"

"Would you believe me if I told you that I wasn't looking for you this time?"

"Are you trying to tell me that you're not entirely human?" she snapped. "That you harbor psychic tendencies or something? Okay. I'll bite. Tell me how you knew where to find me if you weren't looking."

"Radar," he answered in his familiar confident drawl. "It's built in. It can pick out a beautiful woman within a fifty-mile radius."

"Only fifty?" she countered sarcastically, treading water. "Well, don't worry about it. I won't let the word get around. We don't want to tarnish your image."

"I only need fifty. Thunder Cay isn't that big."

She smiled at him too sweetly. "There are other women here besides me. I'd think your radar would have you running in circles."

"You're the only one I've got it tuned in to."

Sabrina felt her annoyance escalating at his persistence. Her heart began to beat in the familiar angry rhythm that seemed to claim it whenever he was around. "That was smooth, Cutter. Really smooth," she bit out. "Don't you ever get tongue-tied when you're dishing out this flattery?"

"Not when it's sincere."

"Is it ever?"

"It is now."

"You've got an answer for everything," she muttered in disgust. Her stomach had caught the restlessness of her heart. Butterflies were beginning to congregate there. She turned and started swimming toward shore. She didn't like the way he made her feel. She most especially didn't like the way he could make her act. In a flash she remembered the last time she had spent any real time with him—the night he had followed her back to her apartment. She hadn't recognized the woman who had responded to him so easily, so vehemently. No matter how many times she had tried to deny it to herself over the course of the last few days, she knew that she would have gone to bed with him if he had stayed any longer. Her stomach constricted, startling the butterflies there into flight. How long had it been since she had been with a man? Nearly three years, she figured. And yet she had been only a step away from throwing caution and all her principles to the wind with this . . . this egotistical, shallow playboy. She shivered slightly, as though the water had suddenly turned frigid. She wasn't sure whom she despised more—him or herself. God, but this Chase Cutter was a dangerous man, true to everything she had heard about him.

Just as she got close enough to shore to find her footing, his voice rang out behind her, startling her into turning around.

"That first answer I gave you was the truth," he shouted, his voice carrying to her over the sound of the waves.

Sabrina scowled. "What first answer? You had a lot of them." She knew she should have kept heading toward shore, but as always, he seemed to have some strange power over her. She found her footing and waited for him to catch up with her.

"The one about how I wasn't really looking for you this time," he explained when he reached her.

"Don't worry about it, Cutter. I don't know what the truth is—and I doubt you'll tell me—but one thing's for sure. I didn't believe the story about the radar. Granted, you're many things, but I'll put my money on human being one of them."

She expected at least a flicker of the familiar sardonic grin that always sent her blood pressure up, but all she got was a thoughtful frown. "I've never lied to you, and I'm not going to start," he answered eventually. "It tends to play hell with a relationship, and if I have my way, we're going to have one, whether it's business or personal or both."

Fear coasted through her at his dauntless determination. It ignited her temper further. "Sooner or later you're going to have to learn what it is like not to have your way," she responded heatedly.

I already have, he thought grimly, but he said, "Later, then. I have no intention of learning now with you."

"The power of positive thinking?" she asked sarcastically.

"It has its merits. Now, will you shut up and let me confess?"

"To what?" Despite her annoyance with him, she was curious as to what he was talking about.

"To how I found you down here."

"Do I have any choice but to listen to this?" she asked, her curiosity assuaged. His "confession" would undoubtedly be another polished come-on.

"You can always run back to work again."

"Something tells me you'd follow me."

"Something tells you right."

The tension between them was becoming palpable. It touched her, wrapping itself painfully around her skin. It strangled her so that she could barely find her voice. "You must win awards for your stubbornness," she bit out at last.

"No, but I've won a few for my resort developments."

Sabrina closed her eyes briefly. A hollow feeling of futility claimed her. "So we're back to that again."

"It's the nature of my confession. My radar didn't tell me where you were this morning."

"As opposed to other mornings?" she snapped.

Cutter finally grinned. "Right."

"So how did you find me this morning, and what does that have to do with the fact that you're tilting at windmills as far as my island is concerned?"

"I more or less stumbled on you inadvertently. I was down here looking for possible places to put cottages."

She slapped her hand against the water hard enough to create a fan of spray in his face. Cutter shook his head, spattering water back at her. Amazingly, his smile held. "No need to get violent about it."

"Violence isn't in my nature, Cutter, although you present a good reason for developing the habit," she responded coldly. "I'm going to say this once more. You might consider listening this time. The answer is no. N-O. You can't have Thunder Cay. You're wasting your time here—in more ways than one."

She turned away from him emphatically. Her heart

thundered in her ears as she pushed her way out of the water. She was beginning to feel overpowered by him, even more cornered and trapped than she had that first morning on the patio when he had so blatantly kissed her.

Go away, she pleaded with him silently. Get out of my life. Let me go back to the calm, predictable way things were before you arrived.

She was about to whirl back to him and tell him as much, but as she reached the shore, the sight of her clothes on the beach hit her like a slap in the face. Her gaze traveled away from them and down her own body as a furious maelstrom of hot and cold washed over her.

She was naked.

Oddly, the thought had never occurred to her when she had been in water up to her neck. She had been too overwhelmed with the shock of his sudden intrusion into her world again, too frightened and angry over his relentless pursuit of her and her island. But now . . . now she could hear Cutter splashing out of the water behind her, and she was standing there so vulnerably exposed. Her eyes flew wildly along the beach. There was nothing to hide behind. Color stained her cheeks; the soft, warm breeze tickled her damp skin as though it were trying to add insult to injury and make sure she didn't forget the awkward position she was in. She hugged her arms across her breasts and felt the beginnings of hot tears press against her eyes as she realized the fruitlessness of her efforts. She didn't have enough arms to cover everything she had to cover.

Then another thought dawned on her. It was horrifying enough to shock the tears from her eyes. Cutter hadn't come down here to swim. He had been looking over the land. The odds against his having brought a swimsuit were tremendous.

Slowly, her eyes wide, she turned around. He was standing a few feet away from her, his feet planted slightly apart in the churning surf, his hands on his hips. The most maddening smile played across his lips.

Some small part of her tumbling thoughts absorbed the smile, but for the most part she saw nothing other than the tanned expanse of his shoulders, the way his bronzed skin seemed to ripple over the muscles of his chest, the way his chest tapered down to the slim contours of his waist and hips. He looked beautiful and virile, rugged and manly. His legs were so perfect, so muscled and hard. Then her eyes fell to the undeniable, unavoidable evidence that he wanted her, that he was just as much aware of her nudity as she was of his. The sexual electricity that made him so sure of himself, so confident, reached out to her, scorching her. It made her feel wired, alive.

Oh, my God, she thought wildly. I want him, too.

The thought was like a bucket of cold water being flung in her face. She didn't *want* to want him, not another man like him, a man who could tear her apart with his rumors, with his callous, heartless bent for meaningless seduction. She began backing away from him warily.

"What did you think you were trying to pull, Cutter?" she demanded. Her own desire for him made her voice even more harsh than it had been before.

Cutter shrugged almost insolently, but his eyes spoke of the challenge he had been issuing to her since the moment she had met him. "When opportunity knocks . . ." he drawled, trailing off. "You took your clothes off long before I did, Tiger Eyes."

"I was alone when I did it! I didn't know you were going to come sneaking up on me! *Damn* you, Cutter! Go away and leave me alone!"

Helpless fury welled up inside her. Maybe, just maybe, she could fight him, but fighting herself was a whole different ball game. Her strongest instinct was to escape from the feelings he stirred in her. She turned suddenly and sprinted up the beach toward her pile of clothes sitting some hundred feet away.

Cutter didn't sneak up on her this time. She could hear his feet pounding against the sand as he ran after her. Her heart hurtled into her throat as she swooped down and grabbed her clothing, then kept running.

It was a useless race. He caught her arm within seconds, pulling her to a stop. For a moment they only stared at each other, both of them winded. Sabrina felt her breath hot and heavy in her lungs as she struggled for air.

"You've been running from me for days, Tiger Eyes," he said breathlessly. "When are you going to understand that it won't do any good? I'm not going to go away."

She wrenched away from him and struggled into her shorts without answering. But before she could make sense of the jumbled wad of her blouse, Cutter pulled it out of her trembling hands. It fluttered back to the sand as he dropped it.

"It's too late for that," he admonished gently. Somehow, the understanding in his voice destroyed her willpower more than any force he could have used.

"Damn you, Cutter," she moaned, but then she was unable to say any more. His hands slid up her arms to her shoulders, and he pulled her against his chest. Even token resistance was beyond her in that moment. She found his mouth almost eagerly, parting her own lips. She kissed him slowly, a vague sense of exploration awakening in her.

Suddenly it didn't matter anymore that she wore only her shorts, that he wore nothing at all. All that mattered was the way their skin met, the way his chest felt against her breasts as she was crushed against him. Her breath caught in her throat as a simmering electricity raced through her at their contact. Her hands found his hair; her fingers threaded through it. It was softer than she would have thought. She had imagined everything about him to be hard, rough.

The more she touched him, the more she wanted him. Desire was an alien force that crashed through her, demanding that her hands slide down to his shoulders, down over the taut brown skin rippling over the muscles of his chest.

He was a panther and he was on the prowl. He would take her and then he would walk away. She knew all that with some small, still-functioning part of her brain. He wanted nothing more from her than a quick island fling—he had *said* as much the day he had arrived to shatter her world. He wanted that, and her island. He wanted a chance to seduce Thunder Cay away from her. She knew that, but she felt absolutely powerless against her need for him.

Cutter made a sound deep in his throat and buried his hands in her hair, holding her still as their kiss deepened. She didn't try to pull away from him. She astounded herself by relaxing against him instead. Her arms found their way around his waist, and she clung to him. His body was hard, a pillar of support that she would have crumbled without.

Yet his hands were gentle, soft in a way that belied their weathered appearance. They found her breasts and stroked along her waist with a restrained care that she never would have expected from him.

She wasn't even entirely aware of his lowering her to the sand. Her thoughts flitted from one sensation to the next, savoring them with an almost childish delight and surprise. Men weren't supposed to be like this . . . especially this man. They demanded and they took; they never gave. But Cutter's mouth was closing over her breast and his tongue was teasing her nipple, and the sensations rushing through her were ones she had never known before. His tongue was velvet, his teeth gentle little executioners of her willpower. She heard herself moan his name.

Cutter laughed softly. "The tiger goes deeper than your eyes," he mused, and then his mouth reclaimed hers. His hand found her breast again and caressed it. His fingers brushed almost inadvertently over her nipple, and fiery tension sang through her. She felt her nipple harden with a sense of wonder.

She arched against him instinctively, the need inside her deep enough to touch her soul. Cutter shifted his weight almost infinitesimally with clearly practiced grace. His hands never ceased in their roamings; his mouth never paused in its invasion of hers.

Perhaps it was the subtle reminder of his experience that first made something tiny and cold squirm in her stomach. Or perhaps it was the fact that his movement had brought him on top of her until he was lying between her legs. It might have been the way he moved against her, making it impossible for her to be unaware of his arousal. Doubt wriggled in her stomach, and her sanity began to struggle to make itself heard.

"Cutter . . ." It took everything she had to form his name again, this time with some sense of rationality.

"It's okay, Tiger Eyes," he murmured. "I told you that you just needed someone you couldn't dismiss with that haughty stare."

His words startled her into looking up into his eyes. They were hooded, their smoky depths murky with intent. He seemed unaware that she was looking at him. The feeling of doubt in her stomach writhed until it seemed to fill her.

He wasn't making love to her. He was conquering her, slaying a challenge. He didn't want her; he wanted the glory of having had her. She knew all that as well as she knew the date of her own birth. He was a man, and men never changed. They sought trophies, not love.

She began struggling against him at the same moment that his fingers caught the zipper of her shorts. With a small groan of desperation she sat bolt upright. The sudden, unexpected movement was enough to push him to the sand beside her. Sabrina scrambled to her knees at once, as he sat up and brushed sand slowly and deliberately from his arms and chest. The look he finally gave her was one of barely restrained anger.

Sabrina was too caught up in her own fury to notice it. "You think I can't dismiss you?" she snapped, getting to her feet. She brushed the sand off herself with shaking hands. "Well, watch me, Cutter, because that's exactly what I'm about to do. Go play your games with someone who might consider herself lucky to hold your attention for an afternoon. I don't."

She had retrieved her blouse and was struggling into it when Cutter sprang to his feet so suddenly that it frightened her. His eyes burned holes in her.

"Hold everything, Tiger Eyes," he drawled in a deadly serious voice. "You've got a bit of explaining to do before you disappear this time."

She stared at him, her face blank and pale. "Explaining? I don't owe you any explanations. The last time I looked at my birth certificate, I was over twenty-one. That gives me the right to make my own decisions. I'm deciding to get out of here before you can call me another notch in your bedpost."

"And I'm deciding that I have a right to know why you don't want to call me another notch in yours."

"What?"

He answered her yelp of outrage with a small, condescending smile. "I'm tired of playing guessing games with you. Suppose you fill me in on your motivations."

"Motivations for what?" she demanded.

"I happen to know that I don't have the plague. What I don't know is why you're treating me as if I do."

She laughed shortly. "I thought we'd settled that. I don't like playboys. I don't like rumors. I don't like you. Does that spell it out for you?"

"No." His response was flat and cold. Sabrina hesitated as she did up the last button on her blouse and glanced back at him.

"You can forget the act on this one, Tiger Eyes," he went on. "I'm not just another guy who's wandered into Thunder Cay from parts unknown. I've been cruising these islands for a lot longer than you've been a part of them. I know when you got here, I know how you got here, and I know what you've been up to since. It's no secret that you don't avoid other boaters the way you've been avoiding me."

"What are you saying?" she breathed, feeling strangled. Who had been talking now, and what, dear God, had they been saying?

"I'm telling you that rumor has it that you're capable of being pretty damned friendly with the other guys who cruise in here." His eyes were steely and assessing. He was waiting for her reaction again, but not in his usual amused way.

Sabrina cringed as though he had slapped her. It took almost a full minute for the cold, concealing mask to fall over her face again. "You're trying to play psychiatrist again, Cutter," she scoffed. "But it won't work. You're not going to goad me into your bed. I'm not going to be another one of your casual, cheap little affairs. Just for the record, I choose who I sleep with very carefully—and you're not up to my standards."

"This is getting more interesting all the time. Just what are your standards?"

"Believe me, you'd never meet them."

"Let me hear them anyway."

She started to walk away, then turned back to him. The wind blew her hair into her eyes and she pushed it away fretfully. Her throat felt oddly tight with unshed tears—tears that she hadn't felt the urge to cry in years.

"My standards are really very simple," she answered in a faint, strangled voice. "I've had more than I can stand of pretty, shallow little boys who measure their worth by the number of beds they can crawl into. Do you know how many times I've heard via the Houston grapevine that I've slept with this one or that one? Do you know how many times my own ex-husband bandied my name about? Enough for it to get back to me that the reason he played around was because we had an 'understanding' and I did the same thing." Her voice got stronger and more sarcastic as remembered pain simmered through her. "But that was all okay," she went on, laughing harshly. "It made our names conversation-worthy. Everyone loves a good scandal. People would flock to Ken's restaurants to catch a glimpse of us; they'd invite us to their parties; it got us into some pretty closed circles. I was supposed to be the idiosyncratic model, and Ken just flapped right along on my coattails. It didn't matter. According to Ken, the idea of a monogamous society was outdated anyway. Well, that's fine by me. You can keep your society, and I'll stay here on my island. Alone. That excludes you, Cutter."

She whirled away from him, her heart pounding, but his voice stopped her again. "You thought that by coming down here you could play your games without the repercussions?"

Sabrina froze in her tracks. She turned back to him slowly, her fury so wild that she was afraid even to move for fear of its reaching uncontrollable proportions. "You bastard," she whispered desperately. "Haven't you heard a single word I've said? Or is it just that you're as callous as everyone says you are?"

His eyes were slate gray and cold. "I'm not callous. And I heard everything you said. You left behind a sexual rat race in a city where you knew quite a few people, to come here where you could have quiet little liaisons with boaters you'll never have to see again. And that's why you don't want any part of me. Because people talk about me. Because you know I'll be back someday. You almost forgot all that for a minute there, didn't you? You almost forgot that with me it couldn't be just a simple little moment of insanity on the beach, a moment you could put behind you and forget."

Sabrina squeezed her eyes shut for a second, trying to beat away the hopeless despair that was threatening to swallow her. Once upon a time it had been different here on the island. Her life had been peaceful and quiet, with no one and nothing intruding to crack her heart open at whim. At times it might have been boring, maybe she'd even felt a little empty and aimless on occasion, but her existence had always been blessedly safe.

But now Chase Cutter had arrived, and nothing was the same. The emptiness was gone, the boredom had certainly vanished, but the nightmare was starting all over again. He was *making* it start all over again. He'd heard things about her, so therefore they must be true.

She swallowed hard, trying desperately to dredge up her best careless, unconcerned attitude. She'd learned a long time ago that the more she protested, the less people seemed to believe her.

"My quiet little liaisons, to use your term, are nothing more than the trappings of a social life," she answered in a dead voice. "Take it or leave it, Cutter. I really don't give a damn what you believe. I'm used to facing up to gossip that I don't deserve. But just for the record, I do occasionally have lunch or dinner with some of the boaters. Period. It has nothing to do with sex."

"Mmm," Cutter murmured, not giving anything away with his eyes now. "I'm sure they're very unexciting, platonic dates."

"That's exactly what they are—platonic. And they're enjoyable enough," she answered stiffly. "I prefer them that way. If I believed in casual sex, I wouldn't be standing here fully dressed right now." Her eyes flicked over him as she said a silent prayer that he would follow her example. It was easy enough to avoid looking at him when she was fired up, but her anger was slowly draining out of her. She felt bereft and empty, emotionally exhausted. The last thing she needed right now was to tangle with the feelings stirred up in her by the sight of him standing there naked.

"If I forgot anything while we were rolling around in the sand," she went on, staring pointedly out to sea again, "it was what men like you can do to me. I forgot all the lessons I learned about paying the piper. You can stand there and hurl accusations and hearsay at me all you want, but the bottom line is that I thank God I finally started remembering before it was too late." She turned back to him suddenly, her eyes weary. "Look, Cutter, we've been sparring about this and my island for days. Let's give it up, shall we? You can't have Thunder Cay, and it's useless to pursue me, because I don't believe in open-ended, casual affairs the way you do."

She was more than ready to end the conversation and leave, but Cutter didn't seem to share the same sentiments. His gaze turned thoughtful. "I suppose most of my affairs *have* been casual, now that I think about it," he mused, as though the thought had just occurred to him. "But if they have been, it's been by mutual choice. I'll be damned if I'll admit to being some kind of callous rogue because of it. Maybe we've been traveling in different circles, but the women I've known haven't wanted to get any more involved than I have."

"Then I don't have much in common with the women you've known," she responded flatly.

"You won't get an argument from me there."

She glanced up at him, startled. His familiar confident grin was back in place. "You're more of a challenge than anyone I've ever met," he went on. "Even assuming that your dinners with the other boaters were platonic, that still doesn't explain why you won't come near me— platonically or otherwise—with a ten-foot pole. You're driving me crazy, Tiger Eyes. No one's ever done that before. There's no way in hell I'm going to throw my hands in the air and give up on you yet. No, I'm going to spend more time with you. I'm at least going to figure you out."

Sabrina hugged herself as the sun slipped behind a cloud. The breeze felt suddenly cold. She wondered if it was some kind of omen.

"That's going to be difficult, Cutter," she pointed out, her voice sounding strangled. "You've only taken your slip through Thursday. That doesn't leave you much time. Even I'll admit that I'm more complicated than that."

His smile never wavered. Again she thought of a panther, and she wondered how painful it would be when he pounced on her this time. "I've got all the time in the world, Tiger Eyes," he answered. "I want you, and I want Thunder Cay. I've already decided that I'm not leaving on Thursday. In fact, if you stop by your office, you'll find out that I've taken the slip for another week—with the option of keeping it beyond that time, of course."

Sabrina felt her heart skip a beat. Its erratic rhythm made her feel almost dizzy. "You've *what?*" she managed.

"I'm staying for a while, Tiger Eyes. I'm staying for as long as it takes to talk you into becoming my partner. Beyond that, we'll have to wait and see."

5

~eeeeeeeeeeee~

He's crazy," Sabrina muttered to herself. She stood beside the office window, one elbow braced on the sill. On the other side of the glass, Cutter paused as he strolled down the pier, and tipped his hat to her.

"A cowboy hat in the Bahamas, for heaven's sake," she went on in an undertone, and turned away from the window. "Why didn't he leave it in Texas? Why didn't he leave *himself* in Texas?"

"Did you say something?" Dwight looked up from the papers he had spread across the counter and gave her a perplexed frown.

"It's not going to work, you know," she fumed without looking at him as she made her way into her private office. "He's just a crazy, egotistical fool. There's no conceivable way he can get the island without me giving it to him. It's impossible! Sooner or later he's going to realize that, and then he'll leave and everything will go back to normal."

"Sure it will," Dwight answered. He stared after her with a perplexed look on his face as she slammed her office door closed. After a moment he shook his head and turned back to the paperwork in front of him. He hadn't thought he was still capable of surprise after the way things had been going during the last week.

Behind the closed door of her office, Sabrina moved to the window and stared out pensively as Cutter waved a greeting to one of the other boaters. The other man pulled a can of beer from the ice chest in the cockpit and held it up to Cutter in a gesture of offering. Cutter stopped and accepted it. Within seconds people began coming out of the cabin of the boat berthed beside it. More cans of beer were pulled from the chest and tossed over to the neighbors. In the time it took to say his name, Chase Cutter had instigated a party. They all talked about him, she thought, but they loved him. Nothing about the marina had been the same since the *Amazing Grace* had cruised into the harbor.

As she watched, Cutter jumped down onto the boat and raised his can of beer in a toast, smiling equably. That smile, she thought, her stomach turning over weakly. That infuriatingly unperturbed smile. Seconds before, while she had been standing at the other window, it had been trained on her as though they had never had that awful argument last week. But that should hardly surprise her, she thought. He had been grinning at her that way for days, as though they shared a secret. Some secret. The whole damned island knew what he was up to— from his plans for Thunder Cay right on down to his plans for her. So much for her treasured privacy. She wouldn't have been surprised to learn that the islanders were placing wagers on the odds of Cutter's success.

Sabrina sighed and sat down at her desk, pushing idly through the papers there. She wasn't sure how much more of this she could take. She didn't quite understand Cutter's latest tactics, but she sure didn't like them. She decided that she actually preferred the way he had badgered her during the first part of his stay. Lately it felt as though he were playing a game of cat and mouse with her. He seemed to be everywhere, smiling at her every time she turned around. There was no escaping him. But while he had once endeavored to tease reactions out of her, now he seemed content to unnerve her merely with his presence. If he spoke to her at all, it was rarely more than a joking comment or a greeting.

Worse, he showed no signs of leaving.

He was waiting. She knew that. But was he waiting for her to snap and give in—or just for another chance to pounce? She couldn't be sure, and she didn't know quite what to do about it.

A knock on her door shattered her musings, and she turned quickly in her chair to glance out the window again. Cutter was still partying on the boat. It couldn't be him. "Come on in," she called out, turning around again.

Dwight poked his head through the door. It occurred to her that he was doing so with a great deal of caution, and she could hardly blame him. She knew she had been anything but predictable lately.

He cleared his throat hesitantly. "Uh, there's something going on here that I think you should handle yourself."

Sabrina threw him an irritated look. "What is it?"

"Not what—who. Taura just ran down to the airstrip to

91

pick up some guy who came in on a shuttle plane. He told her he's looking for Chase Cutter. Says he works for him."

Sabrina scowled. "Do I look like Cutter's babysitter? What am I supposed to do about it?" Then, at the look on Dwight's face, she felt her anger slide away to be replaced by contrition. She shook her head. "Oh, Dwight, I'm sorry. I didn't mean to snap at you. I don't know what's gotten into me lately."

Dwight's good-natured grin returned. "I could take a stab in the dark, but I think it would only make you angrier. As a matter of fact, the kitchen crew has been taking a lot of stabs in the dark—to the tune of five dollars per stab."

"I *knew* it!" she exploded.

"Hey, calm down. It's all in fun. What else do they have to do after the restaurant closes? Anyway, don't worry about it. The thing of it is, I don't think you're going to like the reason this guy is looking for Cutter. I just wanted to give you a jump on the situation before he finds him."

Sabrina was on her feet instantly. "Why? What's going on?"

"He says he's a geologist. He's here to find out if cottages can be placed down near the reefs on the south end."

"Over my dead body," Sabrina muttered. She pushed past him and stormed into the outer office. *"Damn that man! Where is he?"* she demanded, whirling back to face Dwight again.

"Cutter or the geologist?" he asked innocently.

"I'll warm up on the geologist; then I'll worry about

taking Cutter apart limb by limb," she answered through clenched teeth.

Dwight fought a smile from his lips. Who said the marina fell short on entertainment? "He's in the bar waiting for Cutter. I'm supposed to be fetching him, but I thought I'd stall and let you get your shot in first."

Sabrina managed a smile. "Thanks. As soon as this place starts making some money, you get a raise."

"Forget it. There's nothing around here to spend it on. Use it as my contribution to the helicopter fund."

Sabrina scarcely heard him. Before he had finished speaking, she was trotting down the steps from the office and hurrying across the gravel lot toward the bar.

It took no amount of contemplation to figure out who the geologist was. He wore a hat identical to Cutter's and cowboy boots. Two large duffel bags sat on the floor beside his barstool.

Sabrina strode up to him decisively and wasted no time on pleasantries. "You're the geologist who works for Chase Cutter?"

The man looked duly startled. "He hired me, yes. May I ask who you are?"

"I'm Sabrina Caide. I own this place. I also own the land down near the south reefs that you've been hired to study. I'm not interested in putting cottages there, so it looks like you're out of a job. I'll have my office manager arrange to get a plane back here for you within the hour."

"Whoa there." The man twisted on his stool to face her and pushed his beer away from him slightly. He wore a smile, but his voice brooked no argument. "That's all fine and dandy. If you don't want me to study the reefs, then I won't. But I'm not going to just fly right on out of here without seeing Chase."

Sabrina bristled. "You might as well. He hired you illegally. He has no right to have anything studied around here. It's my land."

"So he told me."

She gaped at him. "He did?"

The man chuckled and held his hand out to her. "Denny Webster," he said, introducing himself. Sabrina frowned at him, but she shook his hand. "Chase filled me in on the feud you two have been having. He warned me that I would be flying down here at my own risk."

"And you came anyway? That doesn't say much for your professional integrity," she snapped.

Denny gave her an unconcerned smile. "Nope. It doesn't. But it says a hell of a lot for our friendship."

"What friendship?" Sabrina demanded, but she slid onto the barstool next to him. "Yours and Cutter's?"

"Well, it can't be ours. I've only just met you."

She gave him a cautious look, then turned around to signal to the bartender for a soft drink. When she turned back to Denny, she frowned. "You must be friends. You talk just like him. You've both got the same irritating way of building a conversation around sarcasm."

"As a matter of fact, that's what he said about you." Denny reached for his beer again and drained it.

His words were innocent enough, but Sabrina felt her stomach constrict. More cheap talk bought at the price of her privacy, she thought bitterly. Leave it to Cutter. "What else did he say?" she asked tightly.

"Oh, no, you don't," Denny answered, grinning at her knowingly. "You won't get me to tell tales out of school."

"Considering the fact that it's my reputation, I think I

have the right." She turned back to the bartender, suddenly deciding that she needed something a bit more potent than a soft drink. She motioned toward a bottle of rum, then glanced back at Denny again.

"Reputation?" he repeated. "Oh, I don't know about that. I'll fly out of here this afternoon and probably never lay eyes on you again. What does it matter what he's told me?"

Sabrina stared at him blankly for a moment. "I don't like people talking about me," she managed eventually, but her voice was almost petulant and she didn't like that. Much as she hated to admit it, the man had a point.

He obviously realized that he was antagonizing her. Denny leaned forward, crossed his arms against the bar and smiled at her consolingly. "Look," he responded, "Chase and I go back a long way. It's not as though he's broadcast anything to the general public. He was just more or less confiding in me. And all he really told me is that this place looks like a good spot for a resort, but you're dead set against it. He did mention that you own the island, or at least the majority of it, and that if I got the chance to do any work down here, it would probably be without your blessing."

"And without my knowledge," Sabrina guessed irritably.

"That too," Denny admitted, "but I felt I owed it to Chase to try."

Sabrina took a swallow of her drink. "Why?" she asked, her curiosity getting the best of her.

"Because I believe in returning favors."

"Cutter's done you a favor?" She wanted to say that she didn't believe it, but the truth of the matter was that she did.

"More than one." He shrugged suddenly, as though deciding that it wasn't worth being secretive about. "Chase and I grew up together. I was the bookworm, the intellectual one. Chase was more outgoing, more happy-go-lucky. When we graduated from high school, I was voted the one most likely to succeed. Chase was voted most popular, or some such thing."

She was interested in spite of herself. "So?" she prodded him.

"So you know how it goes with high school. The ugly duckling turns out to be the most gorgeous woman you've ever laid eyes on, right? Chase succeeded. I didn't. Oh, not right away. He spent a good many years burning the candle at both ends before something finally came of it. But he got there long before I did. Sometimes I have to wonder if I ever would have gotten anywhere if Chase hadn't stood by me religiously, throwing business my way, recommending me to others." He paused and shrugged at her again. "So I figure I owe him. Hell, I knew that I was probably wasting my time flying down here. At this point, I've got other projects that will probably prove more lucrative. But Chase needed a favor, and besides, I believe in what he's trying to do here."

Sabrina's expression darkened. She took another irate swallow of her drink. "That figures."

"I take it you don't agree." He looked at her shrewdly. "What do you have against developing the island?"

"It's simple, really," she answered tightly. "I like it just the way it is. It's my island, my home, and I don't want to turn it into some kind of singles utopia."

Denny stared at her thoughtfully. "Is that what he told you he was going to do?"

"He—" she began, then broke off, suddenly embarrassed. "He's never said anything much one way or the other."

"Have you let him?"

"I . . . no," she admitted. "No, I'm not really interested," she finished, her embarrassment making her voice irritable.

Denny stood up suddenly and reached down for his duffel bags. "You know, something's telling me I should stay out of this one. But just for the record, before I go I'd like to recommend that you listen to him. Let him tell you what kind of plans he's got up his sleeve. Chase Cutter's a decent, simple man. I know there are people who would disagree with me, but I've known him longer than they have. He doesn't do things the easy way. He doesn't cop out. It would have been the easiest thing in the world for him to forget about a childhood buddy once he started traveling in classier circles, once he'd made it. He didn't do that. He'd probably make a hell of a lot more money if he turned this place into the singles utopia you were talking about, but I don't think he'll do it that way."

"He won't have the chance," Sabrina threw out, suddenly nervous.

"Maybe. Maybe not. That's not the point. All I'm saying is that if he does have the chance, I think he'll do things on a small scale. He'll build up a reputation, take it slowly and keep it small. He'll still make money, but it'll happen over the long haul. He's got integrity. Don't let anyone tell you differently."

As he finished, Denny turned toward the door. Sabrina jumped to her feet. "Where are you going?"

"I'm going to try to hitch a ride back to the airstrip.

Didn't you say you'd get your office manager to bring a shuttle plane back for me?"

"Yes, but—"

"Then that's the way we'll do this. I'm going to keep my nose out of this one. Something tells me there's more going on here than a simple feud over some land. Just do me a favor and tell Chase that I was here. I don't want him thinking I stood him up. Tell him to give me a call when he gets back to Houston."

"Wait!" Impulsively, she stepped between Denny and the door. "It could take an hour or more to get that plane back again. Why don't you wait in here in the air conditioning? I . . . ah . . . I'm sorry for the inconvenience regarding all this. Look, wait here and your drinks will be on the house."

Denny's answering smile was wide. "Oh, what the hell. I'm easy."

Sabrina grinned. "Good." Still smiling, she moved around the bar to pull the bartender aside.

"Listen," she began in an undertone, "this man is going to wait here for a shuttle plane. I'll have Dwight run over and tell you when he's got one on the way. In the meantime, his drinks are on the house—"

She broke off suddenly. Behind the bartender, on the other side of the plate glass window, the *Amazing Grace* dominated the cove. Cutter had disentangled himself from the party he'd created. He was back on his own yacht, standing on the bow with Marci, looking down at something in the water. His arm was tight around her waist. As Sabrina watched, astounded, he leaned down to bring his face close to hers. Kissing her? Dear God, was he kissing her right in full view of the entire marina? No, he couldn't be. He had to be whispering something in her ear. He'd said he left married women alone, and no matter what Taura had said—or she herself had heard— she believed him now, at least on that score. The other night when he and Marci had been in the restaurant and she had jumped to conclusions, their presence together had been entirely innocent.

Still, her blood pressure soared. The anger she had relinquished grudgingly with Denny just a moment before exploded inside her again. She swallowed hard.

"On second thought," she said to the bartender, "I want every drop that man drinks put on Chase Cutter's tab."

The bartender gaped at her in surprise, but before he could respond, she was out the door. She made a quick detour to the office to tell Dwight to get the shuttle plane back again, then made a beeline for the *Amazing Grace*.

Marci was gone by the time she got there. Cutter was on the deck, polishing the teak trim. He glanced down at her idly as she approached, then did a double take. Slowly, that infuriating smile began to tug at his lips.

"What's up, Tiger Eyes? Have you finally decided to take me up on that lobster? I'll admit that I ate the one I promised you a couple of weeks ago, but you're still in luck. I caught a few more yesterday."

She stopped on the pier below him and glared up at him for a moment before answering. Then she stated flatly, "I'm not interested in your damn lobster, Cutter. I came to tell you that he's gone. Or rather, that he will be as soon as possible."

Cutter dropped the rag he had been holding and vaulted down onto the pier. "Who?" he asked. His grin was wide now, telling her that he knew perfectly well who.

"Your friend the geologist," she answered anyway. Two could play this game.

Cutter sighed dramatically and sat down on one of the pilings. "I thought it might be too much to hope that I could get him past you."

"Then why the hell did you try?" she demanded.

"I just thought it might help to get the preliminary work done as soon as possible. You can't blame a man for trying."

"On the contrary. I'm beginning to blame you very much. This is getting out of hand, Cutter. I don't care how many favors Denny thinks he owes you, the fact of the matter is that you've just wasted a lot of that poor man's time."

Cutter gave her a surprised look. "Denny told you about the favors?"

"You took advantage of him, Cutter. You knew I was never going to allow him to do the work."

Cutter cocked an eyebrow at her reprovingly. "Like hell I did. It was a calculated risk, and I didn't take advantage of anyone. Come on, Tiger Eyes. I keep telling you that I'm not a complete louse. Denny will be well paid for coming down here, whether you let him do the work or not. What's more, I never minced words when I told him what he was getting into if he decided to fly down."

His complacent attitude took some of the wind out of her sails. Sabrina sat down slowly on the piling opposite him. "Why, Cutter?" she asked softly. "Just tell me why you're doing this. You've got to know by now that you're wasting your time."

He shrugged. "Some of the best deals of my life have started out looking like dead ends. The trick is in not letting it get to me. I don't give up easily—not when I really want something." Before she could become alarmed at the level, meaningful look he gave her, Cutter was on his feet again. "Care for something to drink?" he asked, changing the subject. "Beer, wine and iced tea are on the menu."

She shook her head distractedly, then nodded. His changes of pace never failed to disconcert her. But she had to talk to him. Denny had been right, at least in part. She was still convinced that Cutter had nothing to say worth listening to, but the least she could do was discuss it with him rationally and present her view. She had to put an end to this lunacy regarding the island once and for all. If it meant having a drink with him . . . well, she had made worse sacrifices in her life.

"No mai tais?" she asked with a faint smile.

"You'd never be able to climb down off the yacht after imbibing those things. Just to prove what a gallant gentleman I am, I'm limiting your choices to beer or wine. Plying you with hard liquor isn't my style."

"Too tacky for you?"

"Just generally unnecessary."

Sabrina flushed and looked away from him. "Wine, then," she answered stiffly.

"You'll have to come on board to get it. I offered you a drink, not waiter service."

She glanced back at him quickly to find him looking down at her with that same smile again. "I take it that your style includes coercion, then?"

Cutter chuckled. "Whatever it takes."

She got up from the piling, trying to maintain some sense of aloof composure. Once she had joined him on the deck, she forced herself to meet his eyes. "One glass of wine," she reiterated. "Coercion not included. It wouldn't do you any good, anyway. I'm only here because we have to talk."

"Whatever you say, Tiger Eyes." He sounded agreeable enough, but his sooty eyes laughed at her.

She followed him into the salon. Settling herself on the sofa, she watched as he poured wine into a plastic cup and took a beer for himself. Her composure was already beginning to slip. What was she doing here? She ought to know by now that talking sense into him would be impossible. Considering the things that happened whenever they spent any time together, she might as well just throw herself into his arms and be done with it, she thought sarcastically. She accepted the cup of wine from him without looking up.

"Look, Cutter," she began, her voice tense, "let's be reasonable about this, okay? I'm telling you once and for all that Thunder Cay isn't for sale. You're a fool if you think you can change my mind."

"I'd be a fool if I thought I couldn't," he countered calmly, dropping down on the sofa beside her.

Her composure snapped. "I can't believe what a cocky bastard you are! Hasn't anyone ever said no to you before?"

He seemed to give the question serious thought. "Men sometimes. Rarely women," he answered.

"Well, I'm about to score one for the women. I think we've already determined that I have very little in common with the others you've known."

"That much we can agree on."

She stared at him, nonplussed. She almost wished he would argue with her. This laid-back, amenable Cutter would be too easy to like . . . just like the man Denny had told her about.

She cleared her throat, scrambling for a reply. "For God's sake, Cutter!" she finally blurted. "You can't just dangle an affair of indefinite duration under my nose and expect me to be so grateful for your attention that I'll hop in bed with you and give up the paradise I've worked my fingers to the bone for!"

His smile was unnervingly soft. "No one's asking you to give it up, Tiger Eyes. I just think you ought to give some consideration to sharing it."

It was like beating her head against a brick wall. Frustration and a raw sense of vulnerability began shaking deep inside her. She had so few defenses against this calmly determined and self-assured man. Her hand trembled as she brought her cup to her lips and took a deep swallow.

"This island is my home," she tried again. "It's my sanctuary, my livelihood! It's everything to me, Cutter. You're not just asking me for a brief fling to keep your libido occupied while you're here. You're after my whole world!"

"I wouldn't try to take it from you if I thought you were all that happy with it." He leaned back against the arm of the sofa and regarded her with a speculative look. "Are you happy, Sabrina? If you could convince me of that, I might go away and leave you and Thunder Cay alone. But I'm not convinced. Not at all."

She stared at him, her stomach squirming. Was she happy? Not now, not by a long shot. But before Cutter had come along? She remembered the empty, aimless feeling that had tinged so many of her days, and decided that it was a question she didn't want to answer. "What would it take to convince you?" she asked instead in a strangled voice.

Cutter chuckled softly and shook his head. "That's a loaded question if I've ever heard one."

"Don't play games with me, damn it!" Her voice rang out wildly, touched with the panic that was creeping through her.

"Then don't play them with me, Tiger Eyes. You tell me you want nothing to do with me, and then you turn all soft and willing when I touch you. Is it any wonder I'm having trouble taking your refusals seriously?"

Sabrina blanched. Like the panther she kept likening him to, he had trapped her again . . . and easily. "It's not that cut-and-dried, and you know it," she protested. "Okay, so what happens if I admit that I'm attracted to you? So what if life's been a little more wild and unpredictable since you've been here? That doesn't change the fact that I still refuse to become one more notch in your bedpost. I don't share well, Cutter. I wouldn't be very good at sharing you with other women, and I'll be damned if I'm going to share my island and everything I've worked for."

His answer was a slow, disarming smile. "Well, that's something, I suppose."

Frustration plucked painfully at her nerves. "What's something?" she demanded.

"Two weeks ago you would have seen me go straight to the devil with a smile on your face. Now you're telling me that you're attracted to me."

Her eyes narrowed dangerously. God, he was stubborn! "Did your ears stop there?" she snapped. "I said that doesn't change anything. I still don't want anything to do with you. How many times do I have to explain it to you, Cutter? You're not . . . my . . . type," she finished succinctly.

Cutter threw back his head and laughed delightedly. Springing to his feet again, he held one hand up in a gesture of surrender as she opened her mouth again in fury. "Okay, Tiger Eyes. Calm down." He reached into the refrigerator for another beer and nodded toward her cup. "Want some more?"

Sabrina shook her head with forced patience. "What I want is to see you cruise right on out of here. Short of that, I'll settle for a cease-fire. We'll close the whole issue of Thunder Cay and try to be civil to each other for the duration of your stay."

Cutter came back to the sofa with a fresh beer and dropped down beside her again. "I've got a better idea."

She eyed him warily. "Oh, I can't wait to hear this."

"How about a compromise?" he suggested, popping open his can. "If we're going to work together, we're both going to have to learn to give a bit. I'll make a deal with you, Tiger Eyes. Throw in with me on the development, and I'll give you my word that as long as we're actively involved together, you'll have my attention exclusively."

Sabrina gaped at him, amazed. Her pulse pounded so violently that she thought she might actually be ill. "What are you saying?" she breathed.

"There won't be any other women," he clarified bluntly. "And by the way, I don't know if you've heard any rumors about my word, but it's always good." Suddenly he smiled at her crookedly. "I think I've just made one of the best deals of my life."

Sabrina jumped to her feet, her blood roaring furiously

in her ears. "You haven't made anything!" she exploded. "Your ego knows no bounds! Do you think you can just toss me a bone and I'll traipse along at your heels and do your bidding like a good little puppy?"

He looked genuinely surprised. "That was a bone?"

"I don't know what else you could call it!"

"And you don't want it?"

She nearly choked at his gall. "I'd rather contract leprosy!" she spat.

His eyes suddenly became as threatening as storm clouds. "Then suppose you tell me just what it is you want from me," he answered.

"A little appreciation, for starters!" she exclaimed impulsively. "Women have egos, too, Cutter. I never even know whether you're talking about me or my island! 'Throw in with me and you'll have my attention exclusively,' " she mimicked. "What do you want, Cutter? Do you want me or Thunder Cay? Make up your mind."

"It's been made up all along," he answered without missing a beat. "You and the island go hand in hand. I want both of you."

Sabrina put her cup down hard on a nearby table and ran her hand over her eyes. What was it about her that attracted such callous men? Ken had wanted her for her reputation and her looks. All Cutter saw in her was a way to get to her island. She swallowed convulsively against a startling pain that screamed through her in protest against it all.

"You can't have either one, Cutter," she whispered hollowly. "There can be no such thing as compromise, either with the island or with me. I wouldn't get tangled up with you if you were the last man on earth."

"Why not? You could do worse."

If she hadn't been so incredibly frustrated and hurt, she would have laughed at the bemused expression on his face. It wasn't just a game with him, she realized. He really was quite used to getting what he wanted. If he had been anyone else, she would probably have found his relentless optimism refreshing.

But he wasn't anyone else. He was a threat to her very existence.

She sank back down onto the sofa and twisted around to face him. "Listen to me, Cutter, and try to understand," she began, trying to keep her voice level. "It could never work. Just suppose I took you up on this compromise—and the very idea of *that* is a joke—"

"That you would take me up on it?"

"No! I mean, yes!" She squeezed her eyes shut in frustration. "It's ridiculous to assume that you could ever live up to such a compromise. I saw you up on the bow with Marci earlier. I *saw* that whole little scene! Kissing her, whispering to her . . . whatever you were doing, it doesn't matter. The point is that you don't even know how to talk to a woman without touching her!"

"She knows me better than to think it means anything."

"*I* know you better than to think it means anything! That's exactly my point. You're some kind of mechanical love machine! Your emotions aren't in it. You can offer me exclusivity until the sun burns clear of the sky, but that's only half of the bargain. Permanency—and your heart—is the other half. We'd be all tangled up together in business legalities, and where would that leave me when you get bored with me and decide to move on? It's not as though you're in love with me. It's not as though you want anything but my body and my damn island! Do you think I'm out of my mind, Cutter? I would *never* enter into a business arrangement on the basis of a sexual affair." She knew her voice was becoming imploring, but she couldn't help herself. She *had* to make him understand. If he would only give up on the idea of her island, maybe they could reach a truce of sorts. She didn't *hate* him. If nothing else, he had brightened her life up considerably.

The thought came to her suddenly, shocking her. She glanced up at him quickly, her eyes as wide as if he had struck her. Cutter was frowning at her thoughtfully.

"In other words, you want the whole enchilada and won't settle for anything less," he said finally. If he noticed her stricken expression, he made no comment on it. "That shouldn't surprise me, I suppose," he went on. "If you were all that different, you wouldn't be human."

"The whole enchilada," she repeated distractedly. "Yes, I suppose that's one way of putting it. You're not the man to give it to me," she added, more to herself than to him.

Cutter got to his feet quickly, startling her. Her eyes flew to him as he shot his empty beer can into the wastebasket and went for another. It struck her that he was angry. Why? she wondered wildly. This was the closest they had come to agreeing with each other since the day they'd met.

"Cutter?" she asked tentatively. "What's wrong?" Where was this urge coming from to get up and go to him?

He turned back to her with a tight, sardonic smile. "Wrong? Nothing. It's just reality encroaching, I suppose."

"What are you talking about?"

"Your enchilada, Tiger Eyes." He popped open the can and swallowed from it before coming back to the sofa. "You might be right after all. I may not be the man to give it to you. I've never considered myself the marrying sort. I haven't seen one instance yet where that piece of paper made one scrap of difference."

"The marrying sort?" she echoed, her eyes growing wide.

"Marriage," he repeated with mock patience. "As in redundant, unnecessary and not my style."

Suddenly she understood. Her heart skipped a beat. "Cutter, no! Are you out of your mind? You don't understand!"

He gave her a crooked smile. "Are you implying that my hearing's rusty again? Didn't I just hear you say that you wouldn't enter into a business arrangement on the basis of an affair? That you want permanency in addition to exclusivity? That sounds a hell of a lot like a marriage proposal to me."

"That's not what I meant!" Her words rushed out of her in panic. "Cutter, for God's sake, I'm not saying that I want to marry you! Don't be ridiculous!" She jumped to her feet, her heart hammering oddly. "The only point I was trying to make is that we're not right for each other. Your definition of a relationship is a lot different from mine. We're worlds apart, Cutter, both professionally and personally. It wouldn't work." She backed up until she stood in the door; she was only distantly aware that she was shaking. "It wouldn't work," she repeated hollowly, and then she did the only thing she could think of under the circumstances.

She turned on her heel and ran.

6

Sabrina threw open her living room window and took a greedy breath of the tropical air. Distant strains of reggae music wafted to her from the bar. On the horizon, the lowering sun threw pink and orange light through the dark silhouettes of palm trees and sailboat masts. A lone sportfisherman cruised into the cove from the outlying harbor. Sabrina's eyes darted over all of it as she savored the sights, smells and sounds of her paradise.

It was almost the same island she had fallen in love with at first sight nearly two years before. Almost. Now the *Amazing Grace* blotted out a good chunk of the horizon. With her arrival, Sabrina thought, the world she had always clung to as a paradise had begun to fall apart. The remnants she was left with were barely even recognizable.

If she had been depressed lately, Sabrina told herself, it was because of that. It had nothing to do with Cutter personally, nothing to do with him as a man. It was just that his crazy plots to take over her island were starting to get to her. She had been telling herself that for days, ever since she had run off the *Amazing Grace* with the most ridiculous tears burning at her eyes.

She turned away from the window and started to undress as she made her way into the bathroom. Enough was enough, she told herself sternly. If she spent any more time dwelling on Cutter and his disruptive plans, she might as well just lock herself in a dark, padded room. Thoughts of him were driving her crazy . . . not to mention the fact that they were prohibiting her from getting much of anything done. She had to get back to her routine. She had to get back to the way things used to be. It could only help her frame of mind.

Toward that end, she fully intended to have dinner in the restaurant tonight with Dwight and Taura, just as she used to. She had been eating alone in her apartment more and more lately, but that was going to end. She shrugged out of her blouse, dropped it on the bathroom floor and reached into the shower to turn the water on. Even that small amount of determination was enough to bring a slight smile to her lips. It was amazing how little things were counting for more these days.

Then, abruptly, her smile vanished. Just as she was about to step into the shower, the echo of her doorbell chimed through the bathroom.

Cutter. His name jumped into her brain immediately, scaring her heart into her throat. She swallowed hard and shook her head. No, it couldn't be Cutter. She hadn't laid eyes on him since she had run off the yacht five days ago. He'd finally begun to leave her alone. She was just being paranoid.

Sabrina pulled her robe from the back of the bathroom door and struggled into it as she made her way into the living room again. It's not Cutter, she told herself repeatedly. Still, a sigh of relief escaped her when she pulled open the door to find one of the office boys standing there.

His smile was tentative. "Sorry to bother you, Miss Caide. I've been pressed into service as a delivery boy." His smile faltered as he watched Sabrina's amazed eyes drop to the brown paper bag he held in his hands.

It was moving.

Sabrina cleared her throat. "Tell me it's dead," she muttered.

"What's that, ma'am?"

"The thing in the bag. Tell me it's dead," she repeated.

The boy's smile widened. "No, ma'am. Least, it shouldn't be. It's a lobster."

"A lobster," Sabrina repeated dully. Her eyes flew to the *Amazing Grace*. She half expected to see Cutter standing on deck, smiling at her. She was relatively surprised to find that he wasn't.

"Yes, ma'am. Mr. Cutter dropped it off at the office a few minutes ago and asked me to bring it on down to you." His smile wavered again. "I think I forgot the message, though. It was weird. Something about Mohammed and a mountain."

Sabrina grimaced. "That sounds about right." She glanced out at the *Amazing Grace* again. So he had done some more snorkeling. Was he determined to keep catching lobsters until she finally broke down and ate one of them?

"It makes sense to you?" the boy asked, interrupting

her thoughts. "Good. I thought I'd messed it up." He pushed the bag at her. "Well, here you go."

Sabrina stepped back quickly. "Uh, do me a favor, Roy, would you please? Could you take it over and leave it in the sink?"

She followed him into the kitchen and watched over his shoulder as he pulled it cautiously from the bag. She fully intended to eat it. She smiled wickedly as she realized that if she just accepted it, that would be one less thing Cutter would have to torment her with.

Except that she never saw him anymore; he had no chance to tease her about lobsters—or anything else, for that matter.

Her smile faded, and her stomach tightened oddly. "Thanks," she murmured absently, not looking up as the office boy left. The crustacean made a few halfhearted attempts to move around in the sink, then seemed to settle down.

"Stay right there," she directed it, then made her way to the bathroom again. As the hot water of the shower cascaded down onto her tense muscles, she realized that she was more relieved than anything else at Cutter's latest ploy. Now she wouldn't have to go to the restaurant for dinner after all. Now she had a perfect excuse to stay in her apartment. Now she could just have dinner by herself.

And brood over him.

Was that exactly what he wanted? He was so clever. Anything was possible. She was sure of only one thing: Chase Cutter never seemed to do anything without a good reason.

She stepped out of the shower and grabbed irritably

for a towel. After wrapping it around herself, she went back to the kitchen to watch the lobster pensively as it meandered around the sink.

Oh, just eat it, she told herself. Forget about his motives. Have yourself a tasty dinner and remember it long after he's gone.

She stooped down and threw open the cabinets beneath the stove, then rummaged noisily for a pot big enough to boil it in. "Not exactly a kitchen to be featured in your latest cuisine magazine," she muttered, pushing through a limited variety of small and medium-sized pots. The largest one she had wouldn't even accommodate the lobster's tail. Frowning, she stood up again and glared at Cutter's latest trick.

"What's he up to?" she asked it. "And what the hell am I supposed to do with you?" In reply, the lobster began moving toward the rim of the sink. "You can't get out," she prophesied, then leaned closer to get a better look at it. "Can you get out? Oh, damn it!" Grabbing a kitchen knife, she tapped the creature back down into the sink as it began to make definite gains in its journey toward the counter.

What exactly did he expect her to do with this thing? She had nothing large enough to cook it in, and it was too ugly to keep as a pet. Frustration and annoyance quickened inside her. Why wouldn't he just give up? Why did he insist on doing these things to her?

Dropping the knife with a clatter, she hurried back into her bedroom and pulled on a pair of jeans and a light sweater. By the time she came back to the kitchen the lobster had climbed partially up the side of the sink and was inspecting her dish drainer.

"Okay, Cutter. Fun's fun and all that, but this is getting ridiculous." Muttering to herself, she reached into the sink. She picked the creature up gingerly by the tail, congratulating herself on keeping her contact with it to a minimum. Dangling it in front of her, she made her way out of her apartment.

She caught sight of Cutter through the window of the salon when she reached the *Amazing Grace*. Still holding the lobster a good distance from her, she called out to him. He appeared in the door, wearing his usual grin.

Sabrina dangled the lobster over the teak railing. "Here. I believe this belongs to you."

Cutter never even glanced at the lobster. Instead his eyes traveled only as far as her breasts and he eyed her clinging sweater appreciatively. It occurred to her belatedly that in all her preoccupation with the lobster, she had never thought to put on a bra. As Cutter stared at her with frank interest, her nipples tightened and pushed against the light fabric. Her throat closed as she was forced to admit the effect he had on her. He hadn't even touched her, but her pulse was skyrocketing.

"I approve," he stated laconically with his typical grin.

"Of what?" she managed. Her voice sounded strangled. She had to force the words out.

"Of the way you dressed for dinner."

"This lobster is *not* going to be my dinner. Frankly, Cutter, I'm more than a little confused. Just what are you up to now?"

"Well, you know the saying—"

"About Mohammed and the mountain," she interrupted him. "Yes, I know. I'm returning your mountain."

"I promised you a lobster," he answered, leaning

115

against the door and crossing his arms over his chest. "Well, you've got it. I told you I always keep my word, didn't I? And to be honest with you, I'm getting a little tired of snorkeling. I keep catching these damned things, but you never come down to take me up on my offer, and I end up feeding all my neighbors. Next thing you know, I'm out there under the water holding my breath again. So I figured the best way to save myself some energy and keep my word was to send one up to you this time."

"Don't feel obligated on my account." Her arm was getting tired, and her voice was exasperated. "This creature is yours, and I don't care who you get to eat it so long as it isn't me."

He didn't move. He only continued to stand there watching her with that infuriating smile. "Cutter!" she snapped. "Will you please take this thing?"

His response was a chuckle and the sight of his broad, tanned shoulders as he turned his back on her and went inside.

"Cutter," she warned him, "this isn't funny." He wasn't listening. She broke off and climbed down onto the yacht, her jaw clenched. She strode into the salon, perfectly willing to throw the lobster at him, then stopped dead.

The table was set for two. Candles flickered in the center, right beside an ice bucket holding a bottle of wine. Soft music filtered from the stereo system. Sabrina stared at the table, her eyes wide, then slowly dropped the lobster onto the counter nearest the galley.

Her eyes moved gradually back to Cutter. She shook her head. "Why?" she asked softly. "You've left me alone for five days. I thought you'd finally given up. Why are you doing this now?"

Cutter leaned against the sink, watching her thoughtfully for a moment before he answered. "I was angry for days," he replied eventually. "The last conversation we had before you ran out on me deserved some deliberation. I had some thinking to do. So I thought, and now I'm not angry anymore." He turned away from her to check the progress of a large pot full of boiling water.

"So now we start all over again?" she asked, her voice faint. She felt overwhelmed again, and trapped . . . just the way she always did when his sense of determination flared up.

"Actually, I was hoping that we could pick up where we left off," he answered. "Hand me that lobster, will you? Marci and John are off to a party on one of the sailboats. As soon as I get dinner on the table, we can sit down and eat and talk with some degree of privacy."

Sabrina watched him move around the galley, her heart thudding erratically against her ribs. A dull sense of wonder filled her. He was the most relentless, self-assured person she had ever met.

"You're taking a lot for granted," she finally managed to answer. "What makes you think I'm going to succumb to your little trick and stay?"

He looked up at her, his smile teasing. "Trick?"

"Your gambit with that critter." She nodded toward the lobster.

"Oh, him." Cutter turned back to her and reached for the lobster himself.

"Yes, him. I'm not going to eat it, Cutter. I don't want to have dinner with you." Her words sounded oddly hollow even to her own ears. She flushed as he glanced up at her and smiled knowingly, then turned back to the lobster.

"Actually," he murmured, "it's not a him. It's a her."

Sabrina moved around behind the counter without thinking. She took it from his hands and stared down at it with a small frown. "How can you tell?" she asked dubiously.

Cutter chuckled and reached for the lobster again. "I can't. I was just trying to get you to stop hovering at the door as if you were going to fly out of here at any moment. After the other day, I don't trust you near that door, Tiger Eyes. The last time you stood there you disappeared while I blinked."

Sabrina's lips settled into a thin line. For a moment her concentration was centered so entirely on the fact that he had tricked her that she wasn't even aware that he was standing so close to her. She leaned forward slightly to shove the lobster angrily into his outstretched hand. And then she touched him, brushing up against him. The warmth of their contact leaped through her like wildfire.

She jumped slightly, her eyes flying to his as if to find out if he had felt the same thing. They were close, so close. The air around them seemed to grow hotter suddenly; it was almost suffocating. Before she even knew what was happening, his mouth touched hers.

It wasn't a threatening kiss, just simple and sweet and over before she could protest. She could almost believe that he hadn't planned it. The touch of his mouth on hers was light and almost thoughtful. His lips hadn't claimed hers; they had merely brushed them. His hand rested idly on her shoulder, as though he meant more to steady himself than to keep her from moving. Oddly, she was more aware of that hand than anything else. She could feel the heat from it spiraling down into her body until her knees felt weak. She caught her breath as the warmth erupted into blistering flames and licked through her.

Just like that morning on the beach, she thought. Just like the night in her apartment. No, she couldn't think of that, couldn't dare remember. She shook her head and started to move away from him. His voice stopped her.

"Tell me something. If I hadn't sent this thing to your apartment, would you have had dinner with me tonight?"

"I—no." Her voice was soft, confused. The memory of his kiss still trembled on her lips.

"Then I'm not going to beg forgiveness for luring you down here."

"Begging isn't your style, anyway," she muttered breathlessly.

His grin flashed at her. The spell was broken. Sabrina felt normalcy wash over her like cold rain.

She stepped away from him. "I don't remember saying I'd stay," she began, then caught her breath. "What are you doing?" He'd pulled another lobster from the sink.

Cutter methodically dropped both lobsters into the pot, then cocked his head. "Listen. I've heard it said that every once in a while you can hear them scream."

"The lobsters?" she asked incredulously. "Oh, come on."

"No, it's true. I've known people to swear to it."

"You're whimsical in addition to all your other charming attributes?"

He glanced up at her, his smile wide and taunting again. "You think my attributes are charming? My, we are getting somewhere, aren't we?"

Sabrina stiffened. "If I were you, I'd forget about your attributes and worry about the lobster you just wasted. What are you going to do with it when I don't stay for dinner?"

"You've got to stay. I can't eat both of them myself."

"You should have thought of that before you stuck the extra one in the water."

His laughter startled her. She gaped at him as he replied, "I'll say one thing for you. You never bore me. You've got an answer for everything."

Then, before she could respond, his expression sobered. "You've got to stay for dinner, Tiger Eyes. I warned you that I'm getting real tired of playing games with you."

He was as unpredictable as the weather. "Games?" she echoed.

"Aren't you the lady who stood on the beach one day and told me that you have nice, platonic dinners with the boaters who come through here?"

"Once in a while," she hedged warily.

"Well, correct me if I'm wrong, but I could swear I'm a boater."

"So?" Warning bells were ringing deep in her brain, but she couldn't do anything about them.

"So how can you find any harm in one more platonic dinner?"

"Or look like a fool and call myself a liar, is that it?" She glared at him as her temper started to reactivate itself. "You're sneaky, Cutter. Do you know that?"

He shrugged and turned to check the lobsters. "I've

been called worse. Do me a favor, Tiger Eyes? If you'd just turn around and open the refrigerator door, you'll find a salad in there." When she didn't move, he turned back to her slowly. His eyes were level and waiting. "Well?" he prompted her. "What's it going to be? One more platonic dinner or another run for cover?"

Sabrina glared at him. "You have no scruples, Cutter. You know you've got me trapped. If I walk out of here, I'd be as good as saying that those other dinners weren't platonic."

"Were they?"

"Yes!"

"Then turn around and get the salad. You've got my word that this will be a thoroughly harmless dinner. Platonic, to use your term."

She opened her mouth to protest, then snapped it shut again. It was useless. He had pounced again. She turned away from him and yanked open the refrigerator door.

A few moments later Cutter carried the lobsters to the table, then set one on each plate. As he sat down and reached for the bottle of wine, he scowled. "You know, you've got to wonder who first came up with the idea of lobster being a romantic dinner," he said, as though the tension that had just passed between them had never existed.

Sabrina put the salad on the table, then sat down across from him. "Why's that?" she asked, watching him warily.

He poured wine into her glass. "Because I can't think of anything so unromantic as seeing someone wrestle with one of these things."

She sipped her wine, her eyes still on him over the rim of her glass. "Is that supposed to reassure me?"

"You know, I hadn't thought of it that way." He cracked open a claw and held the meat out to her. "The best part," he went on. "I don't know why the tails always get all the glory."

Sabrina leaned back in her seat, her eyes on the bit of meat. "What am I supposed to do with that?"

"You might try eating it."

"I've got my own."

"I'm saving you the trouble of wrestling with it. I'm a gallant gentleman, remember?"

The light of the candles was caught in his eyes. It made them look like small, deceptive diamonds, she thought. So hard, but so beautiful. She felt something hot wash over her and couldn't fail to recognize it. It was the same feeling that had hit her when he had come walking naked out of the surf.

She reached for her wine with a hand that shook just enough to create little waves in the liquid. She took a fortifying swallow, then leaned forward to take the piece of lobster from Cutter's fork.

"Thanks." Her voice was soft, almost a whisper. The mood here wasn't platonic, not at all . . . but she didn't know what to do about it. Something told her that he wouldn't allow her to get up and walk out this time.

Something also told her that she didn't want to.

She washed down the lobster with more wine. "Are you going to feed me the whole thing?" she asked as Cutter speared another piece of claw with his fork. "Wouldn't it be easier just to break mine up for me? If you still insist upon being a gentleman, that is."

"Oh, I insist, all right," he murmured, holding the lobster out to her again. "I've also decided that this way is more fun."

"Cutter . . ." Her voice was breathless, almost pleading. The whole situation was getting away from her.

"Come on, eat up." His voice was soft, but brooked no argument. "Unless you want it with some of the butter?"

"Yes," she answered, wondering if eyes could really mesmerize a person. She felt trapped in his. She cleared her throat and added inanely, "Butter, please."

He dipped it in the butter and held it out to her again, this time holding his palm beneath it to keep it from dripping on the tablecloth. Sabrina opened her mouth and took it. She couldn't seem to take her eyes from his.

"More wine?" he asked, nodding toward her nearly empty glass.

"I thought you were too gallant to ply me with alcohol."

"I never said that. I said it was unnecessary."

"You're so sure of yourself." Her voice came out more awed than complaining. She pushed her wine glass at him quickly in the vain hope that it might keep him so occupied he wouldn't notice.

"I haven't met anyone yet who was willing to trust me as much as I do," he answered matter-of-factly, pouring more wine for both of them. "What's more, I haven't met anyone yet whom I trust more than I trust myself. Either way, the point remains that I have to be sure of myself. If I'm not, no one else is going to be."

"I find that difficult to believe," she responded, watching him take a bite of lobster for himself and crack open another claw.

"What? That no one else would be willing to feel sure of me? Why? Are we back to rumors again?"

She shook her head and took more lobster from him.

"No . . . at least not entirely. You've just got the kind of magnetic personality that seems to inspire confidence. You're the type I'd trust with my life in an emergency situation. I can't imagine you giving up, or believing there's anything you can't do."

Cutter chuckled. "Can I consider that a compliment?"

Oh, God, the wine must be getting to her. She started to shake her head in automatic rejection, then pushed her plate at him instead, deciding to change the subject. "Call it whatever you like. Why don't we have my claws next?" she suggested.

"You mean I've convinced you that they're the best part?"

"You didn't have to convince me. I've been in agreement with you since my first whole lobster." She watched as he cracked open the claws and held more meat out to her.

Swallowing, she washed the meat down with more wine, then leaned back in her seat. "It's delicious," she murmured, her eyes taking in the candles and the wine bottle. "You do have a certain flair, Cutter. Those rumors weren't lies."

Cutter leaned back in his seat as well, watching her carefully. "You're doing it again. I'm not sure if that's a compliment or not."

"It's . . . oh, I don't know." She shifted uncomfortably in her seat, then nervously speared a piece of lobster and dipped it in the butter. Her hand trembled as she brought it to her mouth.

The butter glistened on her lips. She licked them fretfully, trying to avoid Cutter's eyes, but it was impossible. They were like magnets, drawing her gaze. She glanced up at him, her heart skipping a beat, then jumped as he reached toward her suddenly.

"Calm down, Tiger Eyes," he chuckled. "My intentions are honorable."

She would have been prepared for anything, but all he did was draw a finger across her lips to wipe away the butter she had missed. Sabrina laughed nervously. "I don't think we define *platonic* the same way," she managed. Her voice was maddeningly thin.

Cutter leaned back in his chair again, watching her with eyes that had suddenly become assessing. "No? How do you define it?" he asked almost too casually.

"As the opposite of this. As I said, Cutter, you've got a certain flair." When his expression began to close down even more, she rushed on, knowing suddenly that she didn't want to lose the camaraderie they had finally achieved. "I'm not complaining!" she blurted, trying to smile. "It's great to enjoy a good, romantic dinner again."

As soon as the words were out, she knew that they were the wrong ones. Cutter sat up straight and began to crack open the lobster tails. His eyes were hooded and bereft of emotion as he pushed a tail toward her.

"I thought you said that your associations with the other boaters weren't romantic," he pointed out in a flat, careful voice. "You know, for all the accusations you've flung at me, I'm still inclined to maintain that you're the one who has a penchant for shallow noncommitment."

Sabrina stiffened. Oddly, her first reaction was that she didn't want to fight with him, not again. That, and a feeling of helplessness. He was wrong, so wrong, and for the first time she wanted to set him straight rather than run off and leave him to his misconceptions.

"It's not just commitment," she tried. "It's any kind of entanglement at all."

Cutter stared at her coldly for a moment, then rose abruptly from his chair and began carrying plates and the untouched salad to the counter near the galley. He didn't look back at her. Until he finally spoke, it was as though she had simply ceased to exist.

"You mean anything other than quick sexual liaisons with boaters you wouldn't have to see again?" he asked, his concentration wholly on the plates.

"Cutter, that's not fair." Her voice was tremulous as she jumped to her feet and followed him into the galley. "It's not fair and it's not accurate."

He finally looked at her. His eyes were piercing in the dim light. "Isn't it?" he asked softly. "Try putting yourself in my shoes, Sabrina. You tell me if any of this makes any sense. You've been holding me off like I'm Jack the Ripper . . . until I touch you. What am I supposed to think, other than the fact that what people have been saying is true? You know it won't be quick and easy between us, and over before you know it. No matter how much I think about it, I keep coming back to the fact that if we go into this partnership together, you'd still have to deal with me later. We'd continue to see each other. You're afraid to give me both the island and yourself, aren't you? I offered you that compromise, and you didn't want any part of it. You keep hedging on the issue of the island, then on the issue of us . . . and nothing you've said or done is making a hell of a lot of sense."

She took a step backward. Amazingly, tears were pooling in her eyes. A deadly hurt was choking her. She shook her head. "You don't understand," she answered miserably. "I tried to explain, but you just refuse to understand."

"That business about your ex-husband? He and I are two different people, Sabrina. We're talking about two different worlds here. He has nothing to do with me, and I have nothing to do with him."

Sabrina shook her head again. "You're wrong. You're just like him. Only worse . . . more of a threat." She knew she wasn't making sense, but she tried to explain anyway. "I could lose more than just my heart to you, more than just my pride to the rumors that follow you around. I could lose my livelihood, my shelter!"

"Your hiding place," he corrected her. One of his strong hands fell to her waist and drew her toward him. "Just tell me one thing, Tiger Eyes. What's the difference between your hit-and-run tactics and what I've offered you?"

She looked up at him, her dark eyes wide and pleading. "You mean the part about not seeing any other women while we're actively involved together? *How* involved, Cutter? Involved with the island development, or involved with each other? Don't you see that that's not good enough? You haven't offered me anything, not really."

"Ah, but I have. I've offered you everything that matters. If you don't believe me, I'll show you."

"No," she protested, shaking her head in panic. But she made no move against him as his hands slid up over her arms to her shoulders and pulled her closer. She leaned against him weakly.

"Yes," he answered.

She raised her eyes to watch, feeling oddly entranced,

as his mouth moved closer and closer to hers. "Cutter, you promised," she murmured, trying to make one last attempt to stop him, to stop herself. "You gave me your word that this would be a platonic dinner, and you said that your word was always good."

"It is, but dinner's over. I can't be held responsible for that promise any longer."

His mouth found hers. His kiss was gentle at first, but then it deepened. The touch of his mouth against hers again made her stomach clench with suppressed desire. His tongue sought hers and found it. It felt as though it were searching for the very core of her, a place where she would give up her principles and admit freely to wanting him. Sabrina felt the familiar heat begin to consume her. But slowly, so slowly. His hands slid beneath her sweater, and the skin over her ribs ignited. He found her breasts, and his fingers slid over her nipples with tantalizing promise. She groaned softly. His fingertips felt hot. They fed the fire within her.

"Cutter, no," she managed. "Please, no. Don't."

He lifted his mouth from hers, but remained close enough that she could feel his warm breath against her skin. "You'll have to give me a better reason than the ones you've been giving me," he warned her quietly. "I feel like I've wanted you forever. I only have so much willpower."

She met his eyes candidly. Her fear was stark and clear in her inky eyes. "Please. You've got to understand. I'm afraid," she whispered. "It's not that I don't want you. I'd be a fool if I thought I could convince you of that. It's just that you could hurt me so badly. You've got all it takes to do that. I'm scared of you, Cutter . . . so scared."

His mouth lowered onto hers so that he could punctuate his words with a kiss. "Then again," he answered, "maybe I wouldn't. Hurt you, that is."

"Maybe isn't good enough!" She was getting desperate.

"Life doesn't offer any guarantees, Sabrina. It's a gamble. You've got to take your chances. I want you to take your chances with me."

His hands were back around her waist again. They slid across her skin, feeling so warm, so right. She wanted to refuse him, but his touch was electric and all-encompassing, just as it had always been. She couldn't find the words to turn him away. Even as she searched for them, he began pushing her sweater up. It slid up over her breasts until the air conditioning of the boat touched her skin. It was an erotic feeling, and she knew suddenly that she was lost.

She forgot that she didn't want him, just as she always did when he touched her. She ducked her head and allowed him to pull her sweater off, as though someone she didn't know had taken over her body. The garment fell forgotten to the floor as she gave up and sought his mouth with hers.

Her need for him was stronger than she was. In the amount of time it took his hands to find her breasts again, she knew that she had to touch him, had to have him. Her arms snaked around his neck, and she caressed the rock-hard muscles of his shoulders as a tremor of desire shot through her.

She wanted him more desperately than she had ever wanted anything. She didn't know why, but it no longer mattered. Suddenly it seemed inconsequential. All that mattered was that she nod her acquiescence as he took her hand and led her downstairs to the master stateroom.

The sun had long since set, and the room was dark and murky. Only transparent moonlight fell across the bed. She waited for the sight of it to make some sort of impact on her, to bring her to her senses. It didn't. Cutter kissed her again, and all she could do was cling to him as he lowered her to the bed.

His mouth reclaimed hers as he settled on top of her. The moist hardness of his mouth demanded that she give up all of her misgivings, that she give herself to him completely. His tongue was just as exploratory as it had been before, but now it was urgent as well. She met that urgency with a fierce demand of her own. She wasn't merely going to succumb to him. If she was going to regret this, first she was going to go about it with everything she had to give.

When he pulled away from her to stand up again, she protested. He quieted her with a smile as he stood by the bed. Slowly he pulled off his shirt and stepped out of his jeans. Then, leaning over her and murmuring words that were soft and reassuring, he unzipped her jeans and pulled them down over her legs. His fingers traced fire along her skin where they touched her. When she wore only a lacy scrap of bikini panties, he straightened again and looked down at her.

"On the beach you looked wild and untamed," he said softly. "Now you look sweet and vulnerable. You're so many women, Sabrina. All of them surprise me."

She had been thinking the same thing about him. On the beach he had looked primitive, like Poseidon rising from the sea. He still looked powerful and dangerous. His body still looked strong and sculpted and made her ache for him in the deepest parts of her. But now he seemed controlled and almost tentative, too . . . as though he knew what he was taking from her and would nurture it with utmost care.

Yes, he was many men, and she realized for the first time that she knew so few of them. He was always unfolding to her.

Then all rational thought ceased as he joined her on the bed again. She gave in to the urge to touch him, running her hands along his chest, his shoulders, his back. How could skin that was so soft look so strong? The contradiction made her want to explore more of him, but he stopped her when his mouth found the taut peaks of her nipples.

She moaned with a sound that came from a part of her she hadn't known existed. His tongue touched her nipples with an odd possessiveness that made her shiver. Her hand flew to his neck and she pressed him closer to her, hungering for the touch of his tongue again, remembering it from the morning on the beach. But then he surprised her with other feelings, other sensations, and her hand slid upward even more, burying itself in his hair. His fingers had found the inside of her thighs and fire burned through her, its locking flames colliding with one another. His mouth was still on her breast, but his fingers roamed.

She thought she couldn't stand the heat inside her any longer. There was too much of it; it was nearly unbearable, and she needed to fly high enough to escape it. But even as his teeth teased delicately at her nipples, his fingers slid beneath the lace of her panties and moved inside her. She gasped his name as some primitive part of her urged her to move against his hand.

And then his tongue began to wander. She was confused at first, unsure of herself and of him. Then she began to understand as his mouth glided down between her breasts and over her waist, his tongue leaving a path of fire on her skin. His name was torn from her lips again. He slid her panties down over her hips and tossed them to the foot of the bed to be forgotten. As his tongue found the most intimate parts of her, she thought that surely she would die. She couldn't imagine containing the heat inside her any longer.

The fire of it ate through her soul. She knew nothing but her need for release and for the only man who could give it to her. When his mouth came back to reclaim hers, she clung to him, wrapping herself around the warmth of him. Her legs parted and she felt him fill her. Yet still his fingers tormented her, and suddenly the heat inside her began centering around his touch, draining away from the rest of her, building there and scorching her. Her limbs felt weak and empty. Every nerve ending she possessed had flown to the core of her to dance beneath his fingers.

The fire ignited and exploded. Like a wave of heat, it crashed through her. As it consumed her, she felt him stiffen above her. She heard him murmur her name as the wave crested within her, then ebbed away from her slowly. Tiny flames still seemed to be licking right beneath her skin, but they were dying, smoldering now. She clung to him, feeling them take her energy with them as they disappeared.

Cutter relaxed against her, though he still braced most of his weight on his elbows. His diamond eyes sought and found hers. They were less tentative now, more the confident eyes of the panther who had stalked her until she could no longer defend herself against him. His voice, however, was like velvet.

"You were wrong the other day, Tiger Eyes," he murmured.

She searched for her voice and managed to answer him. "Wrong?"

"We *are* right for each other," he answered, his lips brushing against hers one more time. "We're right in all the ways that matter."

For the first time since he had cruised into her paradise, Sabrina had to wonder if he might be right.

7

By morning she had changed her mind. As the first rosy light of dawn began filtering through the stateroom windows, Sabrina woke up with a start.

She lay rigidly still, listening to the sedate rhythm of Cutter's breathing. Then she slowly closed her eyes again as a dull, heavy despair crept through her. What had she done?

She inched away from the warmth of Cutter's body bit by infinitesimal bit, trying not to wake him. She couldn't face him just yet, couldn't talk to him. What could she say? Freeing herself from the arm he had draped over her waist and the leg he had tangled between hers was difficult, and she thanked heaven that he appeared to be a heavy sleeper. As she extricated herself from him, he didn't move.

Get out of here. The command came from deep in the back of her brain, and she obeyed it blindly. She collected her jeans and panties and tiptoed up the steps. In the dim light of the salon she struggled into them and her sweater, then slipped outside.

Thank God she had woken early. The marina was quiet, still asleep. No one would notice her creeping back to her apartment. No one would speculate and talk. She hurried up the pier. She had slid the key into the lock of her front door before she understood that the reason she couldn't see it clearly was that she was crying. She paused in the middle of her living room, feeling confused and desolate.

My God, what have I done to myself? The question screamed through her brain, and she slumped down onto the sofa. Leaning her head back, she closed her eyes. There could be no running from this one, she realized. This time she had nowhere to hide.

Nowhere to hide. She heard her own thought as though it had come from someone else's lips. Her eyes flew open again, and she sat bolt upright. Was Cutter right? Was that what she had been doing all along, from the time she had escaped to the San Diego Zoo right on through to her flight to Thunder Cay? She shook her head as though to fight the thought, but she couldn't deny the aching turbulence inside her that stemmed from the knowledge that she wouldn't be able to escape Cutter. The island wasn't big enough to shelter her from him. She had no place to go, no way to avoid the repercussions of the night before. And there were many.

She jumped up from the sofa and began pacing the living room. The least of her concerns was that now Cutter would only believe more fully that she had been sleeping with the men who came and went through the marina. The thing that shook her down to the bottom of her soul was that she cared what he believed. She cared. Too deeply, and about too many things.

He was going to leave Thunder Cay. She wasn't going to sell him a share of the island and see it commercialized and destroyed. Sooner or later he was going to accept that and leave. He'd forget her. Move on. Find someone else to pursue with his endless optimism and confidence.

And she cared. She was the one who was going to be shedding tears again because of a man who wouldn't settle down. And there was no way to avoid that, no way to get out of it. She couldn't hide. This time she couldn't hide.

She was trapped. Even if she sold him a share of the island and kept him around a little while longer, it wouldn't last. He'd get bored. He'd want someone else. She'd still end up as just one more in his long line of bedmates—and she cringed to think of how painful that would be a few months down the line. If the very thought shook her down to her toes now, how would she feel after she had gotten more accustomed to having him in her world?

She brushed her hair out of her eyes and realized that she was shaking badly. She stared at her hand as though it belonged to someone else. It did, she thought wildly. For that matter, her whole body belonged to someone else—some fool who had fallen into the arms and the bed of the one man she had met in years who could destroy her safe little world.

Her limbs felt leaden as she made her way into the bathroom and began undressing again with slow, robot-like movements. She had never felt this devastated before, she realized. Not when she had come home early one day to find Ken in bed with another woman. Not when she had overheard a man she had barely known telling someone else how he had slept with her with her husband's blessing. Not when she had eavesdropped on her parents' conversation and had learned that they were going to be leaving San Diego, a city she had loved more than any other. Never.

Because there had always been somewhere to hide. She had been able to run then. There had been a way to avoid those things. She'd been able to escape. Now she had nowhere to go. Her paradise had been invaded, and she couldn't even run because it was her livelihood as well.

She got out of the shower and began dressing again mechanically. Under normal circumstances it would have been much too early to go to the office. But lately, since Cutter had been around, she had spent more time staring at the piles of paper on her desk than doing anything with them. Work was backlogged. If ever there was a time to catch up on it, it was now, she thought dismally. It was the only thing she could think of that might take her mind off what had happened the night before.

She was halfway to the door when a violent knock sounded against the wood. She stopped dead in her tracks. Cutter. It had to be Cutter. She knew he was standing on the other side of that door as well as she knew her own name. Blocking her only means of escape. It seemed symbolic.

She swallowed hard, trying desperately to dredge up the aloof, sarcastic shield she had always used against him. Squaring her shoulders, she threw the door open.

Cutter pushed past her and stepped inside without

saying a word. His expression was frightening as he grabbed the knob and slammed the door shut again. He turned to face her, and she couldn't help but see the dark, angry contempt in his eyes. Some of her determination flagged. She closed her eyes weakly, but the picture of him kept flashing at her from behind her closed eyelids. She knew that he had wasted no time in following her. His dark hair was still tousled from sleep, and he wore only a pair of khaki shorts.

She opened her eyes again slowly to find that he had paced to the center of the room. He stood there watching her silently. His eyes were so steely and hard that she felt something cold coast through her at the sight of them. Small goose bumps popped up on her skin, and she hugged herself.

She cleared her throat. "Say what you came to say and then leave," she managed with a trace of her old antagonism. "The game's over, Cutter. I don't want to play anymore. I can't abide by the rules."

He smiled at her coldly. "You ought to know by now that I'm not going to wait for your permission to say what I came to say," he answered ruthlessly. "You know, for a lady with all these devout principles you keep telling me you have, you're pretty damned good at orchestrating one-night stands."

"Cutter, don't push me," she warned. "Not now. Last night never should have happened."

"No," he agreed sarcastically. "Because you're going to have a hard time hiding from me and avoiding me from here on in, aren't you? The island just isn't that big. So what are you going to do about it, Sabrina? How are you going to deny to yourself that last night happened when there's no zoo on Thunder Cay you can run away to?"

"I don't know!" she shouted at him, her panic making her voice loud and strident. "I don't know, damn it! All I'm sure of is that I kept telling you I was no good at casual flings, and that hasn't changed! I don't have what it takes to eat breakfast with you this morning and pretend that last night was just for kicks."

"So you ran for cover instead." His voice was cold and harsh. "Whores do that, Sabrina. They jump in bed for the sport of it; then they grin and walk away, counting their fistful of dollars. What do you count, Tiger Eyes? Scalps?"

Fury blasted through her. "I count the pieces of my heart that are missing! Pieces men like you took and then threw back in my face! Okay, yes! Yes, I ran and hid this morning. Can you blame me?"

"Yes." His response was blunt and held no sympathy. "I'm not those other men."

"Man," she corrected him weakly, sinking down on the sofa as the adrenaline drained out of her. "There was only one, but he did enough damage to last me a lifetime."

"I don't see what that has to do with last night," he countered coldly.

"That's because you're nothing more than a hedonistic animal!" she spat, attacking him out of a vague feeling of guilt and cornered desperation. She jumped up from the sofa again and paced toward him. "Some of us have the capacity to hurt, Cutter. I don't expect you to understand that, but maybe you could just try to imagine what it is to feel. Some of us take things like last night seriously.

Damn you, Cutter! I'm hurting! I got in deeper than I meant to, so I'm throwing in the towel. You won and I lost, okay? Let's just leave it at that. Get out."

"You took last night seriously, hmmm?" His voice was softer now, but his eyes were still assessing.

She turned away from him, shielding her face with her hands. The frustrated pain inside her seemed to have been with her always. "Of course I did. I keep trying to tell you that I don't sleep around. Why won't you believe me instead of a bunch of people who don't know what they're talking about?"

"You make it a little difficult when you slink off at dawn as though you'd like to forget everything we shared."

She turned back to him, her eyes desperate. He couldn't help remembering how they had been so soft the night before. He had finally dimmed the anger there, only to find a gaze that looked as though it belonged to a trapped animal. What had he done? He took a step toward her, but Sabrina backed up warily. Cutter dropped his hands to his sides again, feeling as though someone had punched him.

"Sabrina . . ." he began, but she cut him off.

"No! I listened to you, now you listen to me!" Her voice was strangled. A mass of unshed tears was crammed into her throat. "I *do* want to forget," she pushed on. "Maybe that means you're at least partially right. Maybe that means I *am* playing my own game of shallow noncommitment. But we're coming at it from different angles, Cutter. I'm not like those whores you were talking about. I want to forget because remembering it will only hurt. If I've told you once, I've told you a hundred times—I can't handle a shallow affair! I don't want to dish my heart up on a silver platter to someone who thinks sex is one big merry-go-round and when you get tired of one painted pony, you just jump on another. That's not me! I can't handle that! If I sleep with someone, I think I have the right to expect that he'll love me and cherish me the way I do him. That's not the way it is with us, Cutter. My crime wasn't in leaving this morning. It was in staying last night. I never should have allowed it to happen. I went against all my own principles and now I'm trapped. I can't get out, and I can't stay in!"

"Sabrina, listen to me," he answered softly, reaching out to her. "You're making all your own problems. You're not giving the situation a chance. It's like someone's giving you a diamond and you won't even look at it because you think it's a rhinestone. For God's sake, look before you toss it back to me!"

She stared at him blindly. Tears clouded her vision. She couldn't hold them back anymore. His words echoed inside her head. She couldn't decide whether or not they were just candy-coated lies, but she knew better than to trust them too easily.

She turned away from him, wiping desperately at her eyes before he could notice her tears. "Cutter, you came here and turned my whole world upside down. I don't even know what I'm doing or why I'm doing it anymore. The only thing I have left to hold on to is some vague set of morals that are being torn to hell by my own hand."

There was a long silence before Cutter answered. She forgot that she was trying to hide her tears and looked back to him to find him smiling slightly. "Nothing could make me happier," he replied at last.

"What?" She was too emotionally exhausted to do more than gape at him.

"If I'm responsible for doing all that, then I must be

making some headway. I want you, Tiger Eyes. Not just for a night, but for quite a few of them."

"Quite a few of them," she echoed hollowly. Her tears were sliding down her cheeks now, but she had forgotten all about them. "Until you get bored," she went on. "Until I no longer fascinate you, or until someone else does it more. Or maybe until you have your share of the island and there's no need to woo me any further."

He moved toward her. Slowly, cautiously, he made his way to her side as though she were some skittish animal that would take flight the moment he got too close. His fingers brushed gently at the tears on her cheeks. "You don't know that, Tiger Eyes. Neither of us does. For all we know, we could be looking at a diamond."

"For all we know, we could be looking at a rhinestone," she countered.

"I'm not going to try to dispute that," he answered with gentle honesty. "You could be right. But we'll never know unless you take the chance and try to find out."

She caught his eyes and pleaded with him to understand. "What scares me is that I don't even know myself anymore, much less the difference between diamonds and rhinestones."

He didn't answer with words; he merely gathered her close and held her. Amazingly, her trembling began to ease. She clung to him only because she wasn't at all sure she could stand alone anymore . . . and because he had become the only constant, unwavering thing in her whole shaky world. He never changed. He wouldn't give up. He never strayed from the course he had set for himself.

She looked up and found his eyes again. "I'm so scared," she admitted.

"To tell you the truth, Tiger Eyes, so am I."

"I don't understand myself," she rushed on. "I hate what you represent, but I want you."

She couldn't protest when his mouth caught hers in response. She really didn't want to, and didn't feel she had the right to. Her admission still hovered on her lips; his still echoed through her brain. She wanted to believe him, but she was afraid to. The result was that the only thing that was clear to her was her need for him, for his determination and strength.

He lowered her to the sofa so gently that she had to wonder if this was the same man she had heard so many stories about. His touch was like a thousand butterflies lighting on her skin as he traced the lines and curves of her body with his fingers. Sabrina felt her trembling return, but it was different this time. Now she shook not out of fear but out of need. She knew what those fingers could do, how those hands, so weather-worn and chapped, could feel like velvet on her skin. She lay still, watching his face as he explored her through her clothes. His expression was intent, almost wondering.

The trembling inside her intensified as his mouth came back to hers. He kissed her softly, with the utmost care. His lips were feathers touching her mouth, his tongue a gentle conqueror she couldn't find the will to despise. Perhaps he would destroy her, but her demise would be heaven.

His fingers found the buttons of the blouse she had put on so unthinkingly mere minutes before. With unbearable slowness he popped each one, and then he pushed the fabric aside. Sabrina waited, her breath achingly still, as his mouth moved to her breasts. And then it was there

143

again, that electrifying heat that centered in her nerve endings wherever he touch her. It simmered within her nipples as his tongue teased them.

"Make love to me, Cutter," she whispered, her voice throaty. "Now, right now, before I have a chance to change my mind and remember how dangerous you are."

He looked up at her, his eyes teasing in that familiar way. "I thought that's what I was doing."

Sabrina shook her head. "All the way. I want all of you."

"Ah, but patience is a virtue. Look where it got me with you." He finished undressing her with unbearable slowness, pushing her blouse off her shoulders and tossing it to the floor before his fingers found the zipper of her skirt. He slid that down slowly as well until she twisted beneath him and wriggled out of it. Still his hands found places to linger as he removed her panties. They strayed to her breast, then back to her hip, always with a feathering lightness. When they finally found the moist center of her, she arched under him and murmured his name.

His hand stayed there, driving her into oblivion, while his mouth returned to her breast. It was just like before. Sensations warred within her, but there were too many of them, and the fire within her simply exploded. She clung to him and moaned, but he didn't stop. There was no time for the flames inside her to dissipate slowly as they had the night before; almost immediately they ignited again as he shifted above her. His tongue moved lower to replace his fingers.

Hours seemed to pass while heat exploded within her,

ebbed, then built again. Finally he eased away from her and removed his own clothing. He came back to her and took her just as slowly as his fingers had explored her. Sabrina molded herself to him as the fire within her exploded one last time. The tension within her escalated, claimed her. Cutter found her lips again with his own as the last of it ebbed from her and tension of his own shuddered through him.

It was a long time before he slid away from her, down into the crevice between her body and the back of the sofa. A tiny smile quirked at his lips, a new one that she had never seen before.

Then it faded and his expression became serious. "How can you possibly be willing to give up what we have?" he asked softly.

Sabrina felt her muscles tense as her old despair came back to her. She stared at the ceiling, her eyes misting again. "That's just it, Cutter. We don't have anything. It's just sex," she pointed out miserably.

To her consternation, Cutter laughed. Propping himself up on one elbow, he looked down at her. "Well, I'll be damned."

"Probably," she agreed laconically. She wasn't in the mood to spar with him.

"God, I hope not. I'm just starting to believe that all you've told me is true. You're some kind of treasure, Tiger Eyes. I'm not ready to leave you and go to hell just yet. If you think this was just sex, then it's pretty obvious you haven't had a lot of experience with purely sexual relationships after all. If you had, you would know that that's not what's going on here at all."

He wound a strand of her long hair around his finger

and studied it thoughtfully. She knew her hair was probably the last thing on his mind, but she had no idea what the first thing might be.

"You know," he said finally, "for the longest while I really didn't know what to make of you." Suddenly his grin flashed at her again. "Or of the way you avoided me, I might add. That was a new twist."

"And now you think you've deciphered me?" She frowned at him, her heart squirming uncomfortably. "I'm glad somebody has. I'm certainly not doing such a great job of it."

His smile softened. "No, you're not such a mystery, Tiger Eyes. Not even to yourself, if you think about it. I'm beginning to believe that you're exactly what you profess to be, that you really do have fairly devout principles. You just can't be bought. Everybody has their price, you know. But yours is one of the purest—not even a price at all, but more of an exchange system." He paused, and the expression in his eyes made her heart squirm again. She had no idea what he might say next, but she had a hunch that it was probably going to be a bombshell. That look in his eyes had always prefaced his most outrageous comments.

"I think there's a real pussycat hiding inside the tiger," he went on. "And I think there's a real chance I could fall in love with her."

Sabrina felt every muscle in her body twitch, then freeze. How sincere he sounded! In the silent seconds that followed, a thousand remembered words crowded her brain. Ken. His shallow flattery. His smooth repertoire of words. Convincing. So believable. All lies. *Marry me. . . . I love you. . . . You could be an ugly seamstress for all I care. . . . I don't love you just because you're beautiful and your face has been on scads of magazine covers.*

She sat up quickly, pushing against Cutter in unthinking panic as she threw her legs over the side of the sofa. She grabbed her clothing and spoke without looking back at him. She didn't see the flash of amazed hurt that touched his features.

"Well, one thing's for sure," she answered tightly. "You've obviously had a lot of practice saying things like that. Your lines are smooth, Cutter. Real smooth. I'm sure quite a few women have fallen for them."

There was a rustle of movement behind her as Cutter sat up. "But you're not one of them?" he supplied for her in an ominously raw voice.

"Bingo," she replied coldly, still not looking at him. "I've heard lines like that before. I've also heard that you're one of the best at devising them."

He didn't answer, but she could hear him dressing. Something fluttered inside her as she closed her eyes and pictured his lean body, but she didn't turn around to look. She ignored the faint butterflies in the pit of her stomach and forced her feet to carry her into the kitchen.

She began to fill a pot with water for coffee, needing something to do with her hands. A barely recognizable pain was welling up inside her, one that she had almost forgotten . . . almost, but not quite. Her thoughts whirled.

The silence coming from the living room became taut. It pressed in on her until she finally forced herself to turn around.

Cutter stood in the middle of the room, dressed again.

His eyes were silver fire. Not cold, not angry . . . but furious.

"Keep telling yourself that, Tiger Eyes," he growled eventually. "Keep hanging on to all those villainous stories you've heard about me. After all, it beats the hell out of taking a gamble and believing what you see. It's safe, if nothing else. And we both know how much you cherish safety."

He turned on his heel and reached for the doorknob. A cacophony of emotions roared through Sabrina, leaving her weak as she watched him. She reached a hand behind her to steady herself against the stove, not knowing whether she wanted him to go and leave her in peace or if she wanted to defend herself to him.

She had no chance to decide. Cutter turned back to her one last time. "You were right," he added. "You lose. I pity you. Keep your paradise, Tiger Eyes. You deserve it. I don't want to steal your hiding place, and I'm beginning to think it's insanity to want you."

Before she could even open her mouth to reply, the door slammed shut behind him. A sob caught in her throat as Cutter disappeared.

8

~000000000~

I'm beginning to think it's insanity to want you.

His words chased her, dogging her footsteps for days.
She ran the gamut between knowing that she had lost
him and telling herself that she couldn't possibly lose
something she never really had. He wasn't hers to lose.
He never would have been. He belonged to every
woman who lived in a port he sailed into.

She hadn't seen hide nor hair of him since he had
stormed out her door. Two days, she thought, twisting
beneath the sheets as she lay in bed and waited for dawn
to claim the sky. It seemed like a lifetime. She had
thought that the island was too small to offer a hiding
place, but Cutter seemed to have found one.

He was still there. Somewhere. She was sure of it. She
had checked with the owner of the shuttle plane operation the night before and she knew that Cutter hadn't

flown out. The *Amazing Grace* still dominated the cove. Marci and John had been in the restaurant last night for dinner.

But not Cutter.

She rolled over and buried her face in her pillow. What was happening to her? Her muscles ached with fatigue. She had lain awake like this for two nights, thinking, dwelling on him, on his parting words. Could it have been only a few weeks ago that she had felt nothing more for Chase Cutter than a vague curiosity about the man behind the rumors? How had he bulldozed his way into her world so effectively? She wasn't even sure when it had happened. Once she had sat across a breakfast table from him detesting him. Now she lay awake nights wondering if she would ever see him again.

Probably not. At least not often, maybe not even to talk to. He had already done the impossible by staying out of sight for so long. Sooner or later she was bound to catch a glimpse of him. But what was a glimpse? That wasn't touching him, talking to him, sparring with him.

Besides, he couldn't be planning on staying that much longer. He had once said that Thunder Cay was his last stop on this cruise, and now that he was no longer interested in her island, there seemed little reason for him to hang around.

She groaned at the knot of pain forming in her throat and sat up. Scowling, she got out of bed and headed for the kitchen. She was just in the process of making coffee when a knock sounded at the door.

Her blood seemed to drain from her. She froze, then turned slowly to stare at the door. Cutter? Could it be? She had been going through hell lately every time her telephone rang or there was a sound at the door, wondering if it could be Cutter, wondering what to do if it was. But it never was.

She retreated to her bedroom to get a robe, then made her way to the door. Taking a deep breath, she pulled it open.

Cutter. She stepped backward in surprise.

"Did I wake you?" he asked in a voice that didn't sound at all as though he would have cared if he had. He brushed past her and stepped into her living room without waiting for an invitation.

Sabrina stared at him, her heart in her throat. He was back. Outside of a vague tension she felt emanating from him, he was acting as though he had never slammed out of her apartment two days before. She shook her head, feeling a familiar warring of emotions. She wanted him. She feared him.

"No," she answered softly. "You didn't wake me."

His mouth twisted into a thin, hard smile. "That's right," he answered. "I forgot just how much of an early riser you can be."

It was a jab that she didn't need. She felt it pierce her, felt it shaking her composure. She cleared her throat to find her voice. "Only when I'm upset about something," she managed. "Otherwise I sleep like the dead."

He had been pacing the room, but when she spoke he stopped suddenly and turned to face her. "Come down to the beach with me and watch the sun come up," he suggested abruptly.

She felt her heart lurch into her throat again. Spend more time with him? Every moment that they shared took her further and further out of the person she had always known as herself. Yet she knew with a sinking feeling that she wasn't going to be able to turn him down.

She craved his company again, even if it was painful. She shot him a wary look and tried to stall for time so that she could make up her mind. "Why?" she asked bluntly.

"Because I'm leaving tomorrow."

"I see." Pain shimmered through her. Even considering the turbulence in her heart during the last few days, it surprised her. "So you want one last roll in the sand to remember me by?" she asked tightly, unable to look at him.

He looked bemused. "Actually, I hadn't thought that far ahead."

"But it wouldn't be a bad idea, right?" she snapped. Hurt was making her voice waspish.

"Come on, Tiger Eyes. Don't go getting defensive on me. You've enjoyed the times we've been together as much as I have." Then, at her closed, pained expression, he went on more softly, "Look, I really just wanted one last chance to try to talk some sense into you."

Her eyes jumped to his. "Regarding the island?" she asked. She stood perfectly still as she waited for his answer. The silence that preceded it seemed interminable.

"In part," he admitted finally.

"Oh, that's right," she muttered sarcastically, feeling her heart plummet down to her toes. "I keep forgetting that the island and I go hand in hand. Silly of me, isn't it? You've reminded me often enough." At least he had the common decency to admit what he wanted from her, she thought. Unlike Ken. Could that make a difference? No, of course it couldn't. She must be out of her mind to think that there was anything she could do about Cutter other than forget him. He was honest enough, but he still had the power to destroy her.

She forced herself to shake her head. "It's useless, Cutter. You're not going to get me to change my mind. Why don't you go watch the sun come up from your boat over a cup of coffee? You don't need me."

"Needing and wanting are two separate things. Will you come with me?" he persisted.

God, she wanted to. As masochistic as it was to listen to the soft persuasion of his voice, as crazy as it was to believe in what he said, she still wanted to spend time with him . . . especially if this day was fated to be their last.

She met his eyes again. Holding them, she asked in a level voice, "Why not?"

Cutter surprised her by chuckling. "Good," he answered. "If you hurry up and get dressed, we might just be able to catch it. The sunrise, that is. Actually, I hadn't really counted on seeing it. I figured it would take me at least twenty minutes to talk you into this."

She glanced over her shoulder at him as she started toward the bedroom. "Another classic case of Cutter coercion," she murmured with a small smile. "You're so cheerfully devious. Offer me a sunrise, then nail me with more arguments. Just for the entertainment of it, why don't you hit me with all of the persuasions you were going to use if I had said no?"

"No way. I'm saving them. Knowing you, I'll need them later."

Her smile froze. "There won't be a later, Cutter. You're leaving, remember?" she called out from the bedroom. Pain lurched in her stomach, surprising her again. Wasn't that what she had wanted?

She joined him in the living room a few minutes later. He was waiting for her by the door. With her arrival, he pulled it open and held out his arm. "After you. Let's hurry. Do you know that, in all the time I've spent down here, I've yet to catch a Caribbean sunrise?"

She cast him a startled look as she stepped past him. "You haven't?" She frowned thoughtfully. "Come to think of it, neither have I. I never get up this early."

"You could have fooled me." For a moment some of the tenuous camaraderie they had achieved threatened to fade.

"There was a reason why I got up so early the other day, Cutter. I thought I'd explained all that to you." She paused, and when she continued, her voice was less harsh, more confused. "I'm not generally an early riser. I'm not generally a lot of things I've been lately."

He didn't answer. He seemed lost in his own thoughts. They walked down toward the water in silence, then automatically struck out for the north beach without consulting each other. It seemed fitting.

"What a beautiful retreat," Cutter mused finally. Sabrina glanced up at him as they walked, wondering if he was just making an observation or leading up to the "sense" he wanted to talk into her.

"A beautiful place to live," she corrected him, just to be on the safe side.

"I think it's going to be a bit of a culture shock to leave here and go back to Houston," he went on as though he hadn't heard her.

Back to Houston. Again something painful pressed against her heart. It had been insanity to allow him to get so close to her. She had known all along what the outcome would be. She had known he would leave . . . but it hurt. Badly.

"You'll get back into the swim of things after a few days

in the city," she forced herself to respond lightly. "A few car horns blasting, a traffic jam or two, some smog. You'll forget all about Thunder Cay in no time."

"I doubt that."

His response shook her even more. Chase Cutter was supposed to be a man who forgot things well, who moved on to new horizons and beds without so much as a backward glance. But he sounded so sincere.

He took her hand suddenly and pointed to their right as he pulled her to a stop. Sabrina squinted into the tangled mass of trees there, wondering what he was getting at.

"We blew it, Tiger Eyes," he said.

"Blew what?"

"We're on the west side of the island. No sunrise this morning."

Disappointment coasted through her, making her voice defensively harsh. "Well, it doesn't really matter, does it? Like you said, this was only a ruse to talk some sense into me. Speaking of which, you'd better get started. In another few hundred feet we'll be turning around and heading back. That doesn't give you much time."

"I'll make time," he answered with his usual determination. "Let's just sit down."

"Is this the part where we tear each other's clothes off and roll around on the beach?" she asked, hiding her hurt. "I thought your motive for this little walk was predominantly to talk me into selling a portion of the island to you."

He sat down and pulled her to the sand beside him so suddenly that her teeth nearly snapped together. "Cutter!" she gasped. "For God's sake! You can skip the caveman tactics!"

His hands found her shoulders, and he pushed her down into the sand none too gently. A thrill of fear ripped through her as she looked up into his eyes. He wasn't feeling amorous. He was angry.

"And you can skip the little verbal darts," he warned. "What are you doing, Sabrina? Hiding behind them, too? I'm starting to feel like a dog with my nose down a rabbit hole, always trying to sniff you out. Mentally or physically, it makes no difference. You're always hiding."

"Don't start in on me, Cutter," she warned softly.

"You want to talk about the island?" he demanded, ignoring her. "Okay. We'll talk about the island."

"Don't waste your breath."

"Damn you!" he growled suddenly. He released her, and she fell backward suddenly as he turned to look out at the sea. She stared at the broad expanse of his shoulders, her heart thundering.

"Just knock it off, Sabrina," he continued in a more level, even if not reassuring, tone. "Just shut up for once and listen to me. Will you grant me that?"

She nodded mutely as he glanced back at her over his shoulder.

"My heartfelt thanks," he muttered sarcastically.

"Only if you say something worth listening to," she added tightly. "I don't need your cracks any more than you need mine."

He glanced back at her again. "Touché."

She smiled at him sweetly. "Touché, hell. You've just been stabbed."

He laughed and turned back to her. Some of the tension between them dissipated. "I'll get this over with quickly. I just want to point out a few things you've never let me explain."

"Such as?"

"Believe it or not, I love this island just the way it is too. I want it because of its isolation, not in spite of it. I'm not looking to change that. But it can stay the way it is and still be shared with other people."

"Isolation and other people are a contradiction in terms," she pointed out. It was an effort to keep her voice flat and reasonable, but she had promised him that she would listen. "Come on, Cutter. You know what a multilevel hotel would do to this place."

"Something cottages wouldn't. I don't want a hotel. I want a few dozen cottages. No televisions. No newspaper deliveries. Just a place where people can escape from life for a while. Good food, perfect scenery. An oasis of escape," he reiterated. "We could invest in some advertising in the States, let people know we're here. Sure, you'd have more people underfoot, vacationers instead of just boaters, but outside of that nothing would change. Oh, the existing facilities could be upgraded a bit. Money would be more abundant. You'd be able to make a few much-needed improvements—like that helicopter, for instance. A school and an infirmary, maybe. But I'm not talking about ruining the island; I'm talking about enhancing it."

She shook her head, feeling an old fear fill her throat. She couldn't let him do this. She couldn't let go of the one perfect home she had ever had. "It wouldn't be the same place for me that way, Cutter."

"Why does it have to be?" he asked softly.

She stared up at him. It was so hard to think—to fight back—when he was gentle with her.

"Changes aren't necessarily for the worse, Tiger Eyes," he went on. His voice was still compassionate, still

157

frighteningly understanding. She shivered. "Not always. So what if the island wouldn't be the totally reclusive place you've made it?"

"You'd have commercial airliners coming in and out of here like clockwork," she whispered desperately.

"Private planes," he corrected her. "And we'd charge dearly for their services. The only way for most people to get here would be by boat or by one of our planes. That alone would make it exclusive, limit the number of people who could afford to descend upon us."

She shook her head again in mute protest.

"Just think about it, Sabrina. You really wouldn't be losing anything. You'd be gaining, broadening your horizons. We could still live here six months a year and spend the rest of the time in Houston."

"We?" she echoed, her voice strangled. She tried for her old flippancy. "What's this 'we' garbage, Cutter? I thought we were talking about the island."

"We were. And now we're talking about us."

"That wasn't part of the deal. I only told you that I'd listen to your plans for the island." She started to sit up, panic fluttering inside her. She couldn't listen to this. She was too close to forgetting how men could lie.

"And I told you I only wanted to talk about the island in part." He eased her down gently to the sand again. She didn't fight him. "I still have other things to say."

His hands were warm on her shoulders, stroking down her arms. Sabrina shuddered as she felt herself getting lost in her need for him again. In another few minutes nothing would matter anymore but that he touch her. She struggled to sit up again. "I don't want to listen. I don't want to talk."

He pushed her down again. "I do. And I always get what I want, remember?"

A sad smile touched her lips. She nodded. "Yes, you do," she whispered. "Do you remember that morning when you joined me for breakfast? Right after you got here?" She laughed softly, if not entirely happily. "I knew then that you'd have me. It seemed so inevitable."

"You still fought me," he pointed out.

She stared up at him, her eyes huge and candid. "I had to. I still have to. I won't let you break my heart, Cutter. I refuse to."

"And if I promise not to?" He was moving closer to her. In another second his mouth would be on hers.

"You should never make promises you can't keep," she managed breathlessly. Her hand went instinctively to his chest as though to ward him off. As he moved lower, it slid upward. The pulse in his throat throbbed just beneath her fingertips.

And then he found her mouth. Whatever halfhearted protest she had been about to make died beneath the assault of his lips. She wound her arms about his neck and clung to him, feeling herself trembling at the point of no return. She could never deny him when he touched her.

He turned her blood to fire in a way that no one else had ever been able to achieve. She wanted him. She couldn't deny the part of herself that needed his embrace, his touch. She suddenly wanted to make him feel that way, too. Desperation throbbed through her. If only she could make him want her the way she wanted him. If only she could make him stay and remain hers for a lifetime.

Her fingers found the buttons on his shirt. She popped them free quickly. She was driven.

Her hand glided along his chest, touching, exploring. Her teeth found his earlobe and nibbled. She shifted beneath him, and her tongue found the pulse at his throat that her fingers had felt moments before. She trailed her fingers down his chest and over his stomach. His hard flesh excited her, and her touch grew bolder, more determined. Finally there was a small moan of response from him. It inspired her, and her fingers moved lower, brushing over his jeans slowly and seductively.

"Sabrina! What are you trying to do?" His voice was a growl. She was taunting the panther.

"Tempt fate," she answered. "Is it working?"

"I don't know what you're doing to fate, but you're doing a number on me," he responded in a husky voice. As though to prove it, he rolled closer to her in the sand and crushed her mouth beneath his. Sabrina's single-minded assault on him was shattered.

Her hands became frenzied as she pushed his shirt from his shoulders. She wanted to feel his flesh against hers, had to destroy the barrier that kept her hands from his skin. For a moment she was content to feel the warmth of his hair-roughened chest beneath her palms, but then even that was not enough. She reached for his belt buckle. Working frantically, she peeled his jeans away from him. Her mouth became fierce beneath his. She shifted slightly, and her lips brushed his nose, his eyes, his cheeks. She knew it might be the last chance she'd ever have. She had to explore all of him.

Finally she brought her mouth back to his and kissed him again with reckless abandon. He had called her a tiger so often. Now he would know what it was to tangle with one.

She welcomed his weight as he rolled over on top of her, moving slightly beneath him to accommodate him. Her hands moved to explore the hard contours of his back, and she delighted in the contrast of his silken skin and the grainy sand that covered him. When his fingers began to pull impatiently at the buttons of her blouse, she helped him, torn between the desire to feel his chest against hers and the urge to keep her hands roaming over his body. Her need to feel all of him won out. She was rewarded with a delightful velvet friction as his rough palm came down to cup her breast. Her nipples tightened as his mouth found her other breast and teased the tip delicately. She moaned and writhed beneath him. That delicious heat was building inside her again, rushing through her like molten lava.

His hand slid down from her breast, skimming over her taut stomach until it found the snap and zipper of her jeans. He freed them, and the burning heat of his palm slid beneath the denim. Sabrina shuddered; her eyes squeezed tight as she savored the feeling of his touch, the touch she had come to thrive on.

Yet when he began to push her jeans down over her hips, Sabrina began struggling. She wanted only to help him, but as she slid out from beneath him, the dangerous glare of the panther came back to his eyes. She quickly pulled out of her jeans and rolled back to him. As understanding dawned on him, he smiled. He greeted her return with a kiss that was almost savage in its intensity.

It seemed an eternity before his skin pressed hotly and

wholly against hers again. She wanted to cling to him, but he held her away from him slightly, once more bending his head to her breasts. His tongue glided over her nipples, and she groaned low in her throat. For the first time she wondered if the ecstasy he brought to her could be enough.

When his fingers slid inside her, she could almost believe it. She arched against him. The heat inside her concentrated and built. She couldn't stand it any longer. "Now, Cutter . . . right now," she begged him in a throaty voice.

He obliged her with an urgency that stunned even him. When had he last wanted anyone this way? Ah, but it wasn't a case of wanting so much as it was a case of needing. The realization shook him and made him drive into her almost frantically. She moved with him, surprising him with her strength and frenzy.

When at last she gasped with release, Cutter allowed himself to give in to the almost impossible pleasure of her. She felt a faint shudder course through him. As the fire ebbed out of her, she wondered if the only thing she had achieved was to bring him so close to her soul that she would never be able to exorcise the memory of him. Glancing up at his face, she knew that nothing had really changed. He was still Chase Cutter, the man who inspired whispers. A pirate who would steal off with her heart at the next dawn. He couldn't be held.

She squeezed her eyes shut and heard his voice as if at a distance, so amazed was she at the pain that welled up inside her. What had happened to her? She had never intended to feel this way again. Again? No, this was different. This was worse than anything that had ever gone before. She had seen it coming.

"Come back to Houston with me," he said.

Sabrina's eyes flew open. "Stay here," she countered impulsively.

"Will you develop the marina?"

The pain squeezed at her heart. She gasped. "I can't."

"Then I can't stay."

"Can't or won't?" she snapped caustically.

He sighed heavily and rolled away from her. "Can't," he repeated. "And not for the conclusions you're going to jump to. I've got a company to run. I've got to do something with it. If I can't build here, then I'll build elsewhere, but I've got to build something, somewhere."

Sabrina sat up and grabbed her blouse. The pain was strangling her now. "Well, that's that, then," she answered flatly. She struggled into her blouse. Her fingers shook as she tried to button it.

Cutter grabbed her arm and pulled her around to face him again. "Don't run and hide again, Sabrina. See this through." There was an urgency in his voice that made her tremble even more.

"Through?" she echoed. "That's impossible. There's nowhere to go from here."

"Sure there is. Come back to Houston with me for a few months. Then we'll come back here and develop the marina. It'll be a good life, the best of both worlds."

She wrenched away from him and reached blindly for her jeans. She brushed the sand from them as the pain inside her exploded. Tears scalded her eyes, and she threw her clothes aside again, then buried her face in her hands.

"A good life," she repeated hollowly. "No, Cutter, that's not what it would be at all. It would be the trappings of a good life. Nothing more."

"Damn it, what else do you want?" His voice was suddenly harsh. "You've already told me that you don't want to marry me. As I remember it, you called the idea ridiculous."

She dropped her hands and stared at him disbelievingly. Her heart skipped a beat, then began to thunder in an erratic rhythm. "That's—I meant—" She broke off and swallowed hard. "What are you trying to do to me, Cutter? What do you expect me to say? Marriage is a moot point, and you know it. It's not the issue here. I wouldn't marry anyone unless we were in love. I've asked you to stay. Isn't that enough?"

He ignored her question. His eyes were silver fire burning into her. "That's reasonable," he answered.

"*What's* reasonable?"

"That you wouldn't marry anyone unless you were in love." His eyes held hers, trapping her with their intent. She felt like a small animal caught in the headlights of an oncoming car. She could do nothing but freeze and wait for him to continue.

"So I guess the next question is whether or not you're in love with me," he went on so smoothly that for a moment his words didn't register.

When they did, she felt every muscle in her body turn to stone. She stared at him, her eyes huge and dark. *Did she love him?*

"I—oh, God." She shook her head and brushed absently at the tears in her eyes. Love him? She couldn't. She didn't dare. "What difference does it make, Cutter? You don't love me. And as I remember it, it takes two."

"You didn't answer my question."

"And I don't intend to." She grabbed her jeans again

and scrambled to her feet. Panic slammed through her, breaking through the last barriers of her control.

"Nothing ventured, nothing lost, right, Tiger Eyes?" His tone was biting. Gone was the compassion she had heard earlier.

"Well, we both know how I feel about safety," she snapped, struggling into her jeans.

His response was so soft that for a moment she didn't realize that he had sunk his claws in again. "So stay safe and don't lose anything," he answered. "But sooner or later you're going to have to ask yourself what you've given up." He paused, then pushed on. "There's not going to be a tomorrow this time, Sabrina. It's the eleventh hour. What's it going to be? Will you be my partner on the island development? Will you come back to Houston with me and give us a chance in a real world without rumors?"

She shook her head. She could no longer see him. Her tears were blinding her.

9

He was really going to leave.

Sabrina stood by the edge of the restaurant patio, her eyes steady and unwavering as she watched the *Amazing Grace*. Cutter, Marci and John bustled about the deck, preparing for the cruise to the mainland.

Somehow, even after yesterday morning, she hadn't really believed that he would leave right away if she refused to go along with him on the resort deal. Somewhere along the line she had begun taking it for granted that he wouldn't give up. Once that idea had panicked her. Now the fact that it wasn't true had her feeling numb and horribly empty.

But what could she do except let him leave? She simply couldn't bring herself to throw Thunder Cay at his feet like a sacrificial lamb, especially since he obviously didn't want her without it. Besides, what purpose would it serve? Some of the rumors regarding him might have proven to be a little inaccurate—he could be so compassionate and gentle when he chose to be, and just as Denny Webster had said, Cutter had a streak of integrity and decency. There was a lot about him that endeared him to her, like his relentless optimism and his determination. But one thing about the rumors, one of the things she had always held against him, held true. He wasn't the type to settle down. He wouldn't be happy with her—or with anyone, for that matter—forever. Not once in all their conversations had he bothered to deny that. He spoke in terms of gambles and possibilities. His words had all been laced with a tinge of "maybe."

And she couldn't—wouldn't—gamble her heart and her island on a maybe.

A ragged sigh slipped from her throat, and her eyes burned dryly. She wanted to cry, but she felt too bereft and hollow to expend the effort. Instead she turned away from the railing and forced herself to walk back to the table where Taura was waiting for her. It would be business as usual from now on. Cutter was finally leaving. She'd choke down her breakfast, go to the office and finally get something done.

Taura spoke up as Sabrina slipped into the seat across from her. "I ordered you ham and eggs."

Sabrina glanced out at the *Amazing Grace*. "Fine," she answered vacantly.

"With chocolate-covered spider on the side," Taura went on.

Sabrina nodded as she watched Cutter disappear into the salon. "That sounds good."

Taura snorted deprecatingly. "You'd probably eat every last one of them without even knowing what you were putting in your mouth."

Sabrina wrenched her gaze away from the yacht and looked back at her. "Pardon me?"

Taura pushed her coffee cup to the edge of the table to signal the waiter that she wanted a refill. "Is it worth it?" she asked suddenly.

Sabrina scowled. "You're talking riddles, Taura. Is *what* worth it?"

"Letting him go."

Sabrina stiffened. "Don't tell me you're in on the wagers that have been flying around here, too? Did you bet on Cutter staying or me going with him?"

"Neither," the other woman responded. "If I had bet on anything, it would have been on just what's happening. But being right doesn't do a thing for me. I need more than that. My only concern is you. Is it worth it?" she persisted.

Sabrina scowled. "Of course it is. Besides, I've got no choice."

"Of course," Taura repeated sarcastically. "Well, it sure looks as though you've won the battle, girl. Cutter's going to leave, and he's going to do it without the island in his pocket. But I'll tell you one thing: If you're what victory looks like, I don't want any part of it."

"Thanks for the vote of confidence," Sabrina muttered. "You sound as though you think I should have sold half the island to him."

"I do?" Taura shook her head thoughtfully. "I didn't mean to. I guess I'm glad Thunder Cay is going to stay just the way it is. But that's selfishness speaking. I came here from Miami, remember—probably for much the same reasons you did. Personally speaking, I don't want to see the island turned into a resort. It's a boater's retreat, and I think it should stay that way. But there are quite a few people who'd disagree with me."

Sabrina straightened in her chair. "Like who?"

Taura met her eyes seriously. "Like the people who were born here. Those people who have lived here all their lives. They'd like to see some changes. They've just spent the last month watching a chance for their lives to improve slide right through their fingers. Or your fingers, to be more exact."

Sabrina swallowed hard. She tried to make her voice sound businesslike and uncompromising, but inside she was shaking. She felt just like the little girl who had hidden at the zoo. Everything was changing on her, everything was going wrong, and she was powerless to stop it. What was more, no one was doing anything to make things easier for her. She was on her own.

She didn't know what to do.

She cleared her throat. "Well, if their lives are so bad here and they're that unhappy, they can certainly move to Nassau or the mainland. I'm not stopping them."

"No, you're not. Their poverty is," Taura answered harshly, forcing Sabrina to face a fact that she only wanted to ignore. "They can't afford to leave Thunder Cay, Sabrina."

Sabrina closed her eyes as guilt washed over her. "I can't mend the problems of the entire world, Taura," she said defensively. "I've got my own."

"No one's asking you to take on the world. But you might consider mending the problems of those people you've taken responsibility for. When you bought this place, you didn't just get yourself a marina. You got a whole handful of people who've lived and worked here all their lives. People who depend on you for every meal they place on their tables, for educating their children, for supplying them with medical services. It may not necessarily be fair, but it's a fact of life that you bought responsibilities when you bought four-fifths of their island."

"Has Cutter appointed you his last-ditch-effort committee?" Sabrina snapped suspiciously.

"No," Taura answered bluntly. "A handful of the islanders have."

Sabrina felt her head swim with hopeless desperation. It made her lash out at the other woman more harshly than she had meant to. "I thought you said your only concern in all this was me."

Taura nodded slowly. "It is. The islanders came to me, and I agreed to talk to you because I realized that if all this dawned on you when it was too late, you'd feel pretty damned wretched. I just wanted to make sure you'd thought all this out before Cutter leaves the island."

Sabrina groaned miserably. She pushed her plate away as soon as the waiter delivered it. "I don't have time to eat breakfast," she muttered, getting to her feet.

Taura looked up at her, surprised. "Where are you going?"

Sabrina shook her head distractedly. "To give the situation one last chance, I guess. I don't know. Do you remember that geologist you picked up at the airstrip a while back?"

Taura nodded cautiously. Her expression said more clearly than words that she was sure her employer was losing her mind.

"He was a friend of Cutter's. I spent some time talking

to him. One of the things he said was that I should consider giving Cutter the chance to talk. Maybe he was right.''

Taura watched, wide-eyed, as Sabrina strode off the patio. A slow, doubtful grin curved her mouth before she shrugged and turned back to her breakfast.

Taura's words whirled through Sabrina's brain as she went to find Cutter. The last thing in the world she needed at this point was a guilt trip, but whether she needed it or not, her general manager had given it to her. Why couldn't anyone understand that so much more was at issue than the island at this point? Why couldn't anyone see that she was losing, too, but that there was nothing she could do about it?

Nothing . . . except perhaps to give Cutter one last chance to tell her—and convince her—that their relationship wouldn't be a matter of two ships passing in the night. Her heart squeezed painfully into her throat as she realized again that that was exactly what she planned to do. But for the islanders . . . or for herself?

She felt as though she were trapped in the plot of a bad movie as she reached the pier and stopped in front of the *Amazing Grace.* Marci and John mumbled vague greetings, then disappeared into the salon. Cutter searched her face for a silent moment before he climbed down onto the pier. His eyes seared her, just as they always did. Her blood raced and her skin felt hot.

"I . . . ah . . ." She paused to clear her throat. It was difficult. Her heart was lodged there. "I didn't want to let you leave without saying goodbye," she managed finally.

"We said that yesterday, Tiger Eyes." His voice rang with finality. It scared her.

Still, she managed to nod despite the fact that her determination was shriveling inside her. "I know, but . . . but that was yesterday," she answered inanely.

"Did you want anything else?" he asked coldly. When she didn't answer, he continued, "To tell me that you've changed your mind, for instance?"

"About the island?"

"What else?" There was a ring of sarcasm to his voice.

Her throat ached as she shook her head. Every emotion she possessed had squeezed in there with her heart. She gave him a pleading look. "Why can't you just understand?"

"Maybe I do. We won't know until you tell me what it is I'm supposed to be understanding."

"That it's not just a matter of the island anymore!" she blurted. "It's a matter of us, of you. I just can't live with the kind of relationship you expect from me." She paused, taking a deep, steadying breath. "That's really the crux of the matter, you know. That's what all this boils down to. Not what you want to do with the island. What you would do to me. Cutter, you don't even want me unless I come part and parcel with the land!"

Cutter's gaze was shuttered. It gave nothing away. "Suppose you tell me about this relationship I expect from you," he said at length.

Frustration and despair ripped through her. He was going to be difficult and evasive, as always. Why had she allowed herself to hope for anything else? "I can't believe you want to go into all that again," she answered raggedly. "We've talked about nothing else for weeks!"

Cutter shrugged. "I've got plenty of time to get to Fort Lauderdale. Tell me again."

She had to choke back the sarcastic response in her

throat. Not now, she warned herself. There was too much at stake. She had made up her mind that she was going to give him the chance to dispute her fears, and she was going to do it.

"Okay," she began tightly. "Okay, one more time. I'm scared to death that all you want from me is a temporary affair. Every gut instinct I possess is telling me that sooner or later you'd get tired of this exclusivity you've talked about and move on to someone else who doesn't mind your bed-hopping." Her words began coming faster as emotion and adrenaline raced through her. "If I were tied up with you in a partnership when that happened, it would kill me. There are a lot of reasons why I don't want to sell to you, but that's the biggest." She finished and took a long, shaky breath.

Cutter nodded perfunctorily. Sabrina felt her heart shrink, then drop down into the pit of her stomach. She felt empty, weak. Foreboding clutched at her. "That's it?" she asked in a strangled voice. "You're just going to stand there and nod at me? You're not going to argue the point?"

"Would you believe me if I did?"

She opened her mouth to answer, then squeezed her eyes shut. She shook her head dully. "I—no. Probably not," she whispered. Even her breath seemed to have left her. "I guess I'd be afraid that you were willing to say anything just to get the island."

She opened her eyes again to find Cutter smiling at her coldly. "That's right," he answered. "I keep forgetting what a mercenary, lying louse I'm supposed to be." He turned and climbed up on the yacht again. "Goodbye, Tiger Eyes. If you ever change your mind, you know where to find me. You've got my address on those registration forms I filled out for the slip. Just cut us both a break and don't bother me unless you have something new to say."

Marci and John reappeared as though he had given them some invisible cue. Moments later the throbbing growl of the yacht's engines filled the air, and the couple threw off the lines. Sabrina sat down listlessly on the nearest piling. Long after the *Amazing Grace* had disappeared, anguish rolled through her like the low waves the yacht left in its wake.

He was gone.

As the days drifted by after his departure, Sabrina came to realize that, even in his absence, Cutter was rearranging her world. It was as though he were an invisible puppeteer pulling strings to affect her daily activities. His ghost haunted her; but worse, the repercussions of his stay on Thunder Cay made his ghost too formidable to be slain. She had once thought that his departure would cure all her woes. Now she was beginning to think that they were just starting.

Her first impulse—which hit her as early as the morning he left—was to throw herself into her work. The marina never operated all that smoothly; lately it had been hitting more snags than usual, largely due to her neglect. Her thoughts had been so consumed by Cutter that she had had very little energy left with which to cope with the problems of the business. But Cutter was gone now, and life on Thunder Cay went on. The marina needed her, and she tried to throw herself fully into its operation.

But it didn't work. Within days it became evident that Taura hadn't underestimated the islanders' reaction to her tug-of-war with Chase Cutter. Problems that had been molehills before became mountains. Morale was low. The attitudes of most of her employees became grudging, to say the least. Where they had once blamed fate for their lot in life, now they blamed her. Sabrina felt cornered and desperate. She could see no way out, no way to appease them. Worse, her sympathies for their position weren't what they might have been under different circumstances. When Cutter left, he had destroyed their hopes. But he had also destroyed her flimsy content with her world. She couldn't cry for them; she was too busy coping with her own pain.

She began to spend more and more time with Dwight and Taura. They were the only people on the island who seemed to have forgotten Cutter's visit as though it had never been. She found a sanctuary in their friendship now that she had once derived simply from living on the island. Her pleasure in that seemed to be gone, but Dwight and Taura were still there to bolster her spirits, at least as much as anyone could.

"It's called maturity," she told Taura in a dull voice one night after dinner. She sat in the corner of the other woman's sofa, her feet curled up beneath her as she clutched a glass of wine in her hands. Taura watched her sympathetically from the other end. Dwight sat silently in a nearby rocking chair. Neither of them answered her. They had learned weeks ago that it would be futile. Sabrina wouldn't hear them. She seemed to hear nothing but the chaos of her own thoughts these days. Toward that end, the pair did the only thing they could do for her. They listened. And they adjusted to the new boundaries of their friendship. While Cutter had been around, Sabrina had more or less kept to herself. Now she had been seeking them out almost constantly. Their meals together at the restaurant had evolved into meals at their respective homes, where they could talk more freely. Or rather, Taura thought, where Sabrina could talk. She wondered guiltily if she had brought all this on with that last effort to talk Sabrina into selling the island. Almost imperceptibly, she shook her head. Sabrina hadn't been herself since Chase Cutter first sailed into the cove.

"Sooner or later you just hit a point in your life where the most important thing is to be true to yourself," Sabrina went on, staring down into her wine. Taura knew that she and Dwight might not even have existed for all her boss was aware of them. She was talking to herself, obviously trying to convince herself.

"I guess maybe it has something to do with taking your lumps along the way," Sabrina continued vacantly. "Sooner or later you just get to the point where, no matter how much the consequences hurt, you've got to do what's best for yourself. You know that the alternative is to hurt more." Suddenly she looked up at Taura. "Does that make sense?"

Taura nodded slowly, carefully. It was Dwight who ventured a response.

"Self-preservation," he supplied. "The question is, can it be taken too far? When do you stop being wise and taking care of yourself and start being a coward who has nothing to show for your lumps?"

Taura shot him a warning look, but it was too late. Sabrina scrambled to her feet as though he had slapped her. From behind her, Dwight shot Taura a shrug and a look that said, "Somebody had to say it."

Sabrina didn't see him, nor did she notice Taura's answering scowl. "I haven't the vaguest idea," she answered his question shortly. "And it's hardly fair of me to keep the two of you up all night discussing philosophy. We've got a big day tomorrow. The accountant's coming in again, isn't he?" she asked, looking down at Taura.

"He was here three days ago," the other woman reminded her gently.

"Oh, that's right." She squeezed her eyes shut for a moment, dwelling desperately on the forgetfulness that had been dogging her lately. Was that Cutter's doing, too? she wondered wildly, then forced her eyes open again. "Well, anyway, I'm still not going to keep you up all night. I'm going to head on home."

"Me too." Dwight stood up and stretched. The three walked together to the door. "Do you want me to drop you off?" he asked Sabrina. He maintained a little dune buggy because his house was all the way out near the airstrip.

Sabrina shook her head. "No, thanks. It's not that far back to the marina, and the walk will do me good."

"Whatever you say." He climbed into the dune buggy and the engine turned over, shattering the silence of the night air. "See you two tomorrow."

Sabrina had already taken several mechanical steps down the dirt road that led back to the marina. At the sound of Dwight's voice she turned back and waved, then added, "Thanks for the hospitality, Taura."

"Don't worry about it. You'll get your turn." The other woman closed her door slowly, and Dwight drove off. Sabrina found herself alone again in the balmy night.

A familiar iciness spread through her stomach as she started to walk again. The only thing that even began to counteract it was company, and now she had lost even that.

She didn't want to be alone. She couldn't be alone. But there was nowhere else to go. The bar would be closed by now, and just as she had said, she couldn't keep Dwight and Taura up all night. No, she had to go home. It was time to try to sleep again.

But the minute she stepped through her apartment door, his memory burned through her mind. Cutter. She couldn't help seeing him: his determined eyes as he paced her living room floor; his quick grin as he realized that he would have his way and she would go to the beach with him. The accusing glances he had been capable of throwing at her when he stood by her door, prepared to storm out. And his gentleness, his care, as they had made love on the sofa. Cutter. God, would she ever get away from the memory of him? It had been two weeks—*two weeks*—since the *Amazing Grace* had cruised away from Thunder Cay, and she still couldn't forget a single detail of his face, his eyes. She still remembered what it was to be touched by him. He was haunting her.

She loved him.

A shudder passed through her as she admitted that to herself for what felt like the thousandth time. Her hands shook as she made her way into the kitchen and poured herself another glass of wine to supplement the one she had had at Taura's house. Sometimes it dulled the agony. Sometimes it made her sleep.

She closed her eyes and could almost see the imprint of their footsteps in the sand again. That morning when they had gone down to the beach to catch the sunrise that never was, he had asked her if she had loved him. And she had known it then, in some dark part of her soul.

But she had hidden from the knowledge, just the way he had always accused her of doing. He had known her so well!

She hadn't told him that she loved him because she had been afraid to admit it to herself. Admitting it would have meant acknowledging what was right around the corner . . . this emptiness, this acute sense of loss. And so, even though she hadn't actually been able to go anywhere to hide from him, she had run from him all the same. Denying what she felt for him. Avoiding him. Letting him leave.

Letting him leave. He was gone. And the emptiness and loss had come. They filled her. She had forgotten what it was like to live without them.

She filled her wine glass a second time and wandered over to the window. The obsidian darkness of early morning pressed against the glass. She couldn't see all that much of her paradise—just the shadow of a sailboat mast that was darker than the sky, the milky transparency of moonlight on the water—but it didn't make any difference. It wasn't her paradise anymore. Had it ever really been?

Dwight's voice came back to her, an insidious reminder of what she had done to herself. When do you stop being wise and taking care of yourself and start being a coward who has nothing to show for your lumps?

She had nothing to show for her lumps. She had nursed them so skillfully that they were all she had left. Thunder Cay had become a prison. And Cutter was gone.

She tossed her wine back suddenly. Those lumps would be painfully tender and unbearable whether she accepted Cutter on his terms or not. But if she did accept him on his terms, then she would at least have something to show for them. Not much, but something. It was better than nothing at all.

She had to go after him. She had to give him the island. She couldn't keep living like this.

A burst of adrenaline hit her, the first real energy she had felt in weeks. She went to the telephone and dialed Dwight's number, praying that he hadn't gone to bed yet. He answered on the second ring.

"It's Sabrina," she announced without preliminaries. "Can you meet me at the office?"

His response was immediate and not at all surprised. "You want to go to Houston? Thank God. I wasn't sure how many more late nights like this I could stand. Is fifteen minutes all right?"

A subtle, still peace settled over her now that she had made a decision. "Sure. And thank you," she whispered. "Dwight . . . hurry."

She hung up and went into the bedroom to throw some clothes into a suitcase. Exactly fifteen minutes later she dropped it in front of the office door and began digging through her purse for her keys. This was madness and she knew it. They'd probably never get a shuttle plane to come in at this hour of the night. But she had to try.

Dwight arrived just as she let herself in the door. While he tried to get the shuttle plane operator on the phone, she dug through the files for Cutter's address. It seemed like an eternity before Dwight turned around and covered the mouthpiece with his hand.

"This is going to cost you a fortune," he whispered. "He'll take you to Fort Lauderdale, but it's going to mean your life savings. Are you sure you don't want to wait until morning?"

Sabrina shook her head. "Right now," she said. "Before I chicken out."

A few minutes later he hung up the telephone. "He'll be here in about an hour," he reported, then started dialing again.

Finally he replaced the phone once and for all. "Okay, you're all set. Go to the Transcon ticket counter when you get to Fort Lauderdale; your ticket will be there waiting for you. You'll be going all night, Sabrina. You're going to have to change planes in Atlanta. Now, let's grab that suitcase and get you down to the airfield."

Sabrina grabbed the suitcase and hefted it against her side. "That," she told him emphatically, "is the nicest thing anyone's said to me in two weeks."

Maybe, just maybe, he would eventually come to love her, too. Maybe this wasn't emotional suicide. Maybe their relationship would evolve into more than just a tenuous business deal between lovers.

Maybe. It was a gamble she had to take. She couldn't even think what would happen if he got tired of being faithful to her and she still had to deal with him on the development of the marina.

It was nine-thirty in the morning when she got off the plane in Houston. She found a cab and gave the driver Cutter's address, then collapsed against the seat. Her eyes burned dryly with fatigue, and her muscles ached. She was exhausted. She tried to think what she would say to Cutter when she saw him, but her mind wouldn't function.

"You sure this is the place you want, lady?" The

cabdriver's voice startled her out of her drowsy reverie. Sabrina sat up straight and blinked at the building in front of them.

It was clearly a hotel, but the source of the cabbie's skepticism was obvious. It was still under construction. The place was crawling with men who shouted to each other busily.

"This is it," she answered. "Do me a favor and wait here a minute. I'll leave my suitcase with you."

She pushed open the door and stood up on shaky legs. The feeling of peace spread within her, even if it was a bit tenuous. She stared up at the hotel. It wasn't nearly as ostentatious and commercial as she would have thought. It looked more like a sprawling white manor house. She could only pray that Cutter's taste wouldn't change when he got his hands on Thunder Cay.

Then all thoughts of the island drained out of her mind. For a moment it was blank; then panic surged through her. Cutter was striding across the gravel lot purposefully, a set of blueprints rolled up in his hand. He wore a hard hat and his face was averted from her, but she knew it was he. That body, that walk had been haunting her for weeks.

Suddenly he stopped moving. It was almost as though she had broadcast her presence over a loudspeaker. Cutter turned slowly in her direction, finally trapping her again with his smoky eyes.

She had half expected to be greeted by that wide grin she had come to know so well. Instead he looked shocked, not like a man with victory at his fingertips. He stared at her enigmatically for a long while before he finally began moving toward her. Sabrina felt her limbs weaken to the point where she wasn't at all sure that her legs would hold her.

"Sabrina," he said emptily, striding up to her.

Her world darkened. This wasn't what she had expected. She cleared her throat and launched into her old defensive sarcasm. "Please, don't be so effusive about this. You're embarrassing me."

He scowled dangerously. "What do you want me to say? I sure wasn't going to put money on the probability of you following me back here. I wouldn't even have put money on getting a phone call from you."

"You've replaced me already?"

His response was a growl that made her flinch. She started to turn away, but he caught her with an iron grip around her wrist. "Not so fast, Tiger Eyes. You've come too far to run away this time." Suddenly his voice was soft and intimate again, the way she remembered it. It soothed the turmoil boiling within her, if only slightly.

He released her wrist. "Stay put. You'd better be here when I get back." His voice was still gentle, but it brooked no argument. He walked over to the cab, paid off the driver, then took her suitcase from the trunk before she even knew what he was doing. He was back a second later, reaching for her arm again.

"There. Now I know you can't get too far while my back's turned." If his voice was still gentle, his touch belied it. He pulled her along roughly, almost violently, as they entered the massive front doors of the half-finished hotel.

She forced herself to meet his eyes, her heart thundering beneath her ribs. "Your surprise baffles me, Cutter," she managed, her voice tremulous with nerves. "From what I understood, all your women are willing to follow you halfway around the world to give you what you want."

"What I want." Cutter chuckled. There was little humor in the sound. "Okay, so a few women might have done that," he allowed harshly, but then his voice was suddenly soft again. "They gave me what I wanted, Tiger Eyes, but no one ever gave me what I needed until you came along."

Her heart lurched. She forced herself to swallow despite the dryness in her throat. "Well, I'm fully pre- pared to do that," she answered. "I'm giving you half interest in the marina, Cutter. You can go ahead with your plans."

He pulled her into his arms abruptly. Sabrina gasped with surprise, then buried her face against his throat. This was what she had come for, what she needed. His touch, his embrace . . . for as long as he would give them to her. Tears of relief scalded her eyes, but she forced them back at the sound of his voice. Blinking furiously, she looked up at him again.

"That's it," he said, catching her chin with his strong hand so that she couldn't look away. "Look at me. I want to make sure that you understand this. You've got everything all wrong, Tiger Eyes."

"Wrong?" she squeaked, sudden fear gripping her stomach.

"Wrong," he reiterated. "There are a dozen islands I could have used for my resort. I only chose Thunder Cay because I decided I wanted you. I don't need your island, Sabrina. I need you, what we had down there. I need you for my wife."

She stared at him, her face blank. Amazement raced

through her, and her eyes widened. Her voice was a gasp. "Wife? You want to marry me?"

He chuckled at her astonishment. "I've wanted to marry you virtually from the time you first planted the idea in my head on the boat that afternoon."

"Thanks for letting me in on it. I let you go because . . . But you never said that you . . . Damn you, Cutter!" Tears fought through her laughter.

He placed a calloused finger against her lips. "Whoa. Cutter's the guy you heard all those rumors about. He doesn't exist. I'm Chase. And I'm only a man, not some crazy legend. I wasn't going to risk my heart until I knew for sure that you wanted me, too. Really wanted me, for longer than it took to take a walk on the beach. I couldn't be sure."

"So you let me suffer," she muttered. The smile on her lips widened. It was fueled by a wild, ecstatic churning deep inside her.

Cutter shrugged in that special way he had. His familiar grin quirked at his mouth. "I knew if you followed me back to Houston, if you were willing to leave your little island for me, then I was safe." Suddenly his expression turned serious again. "I'm not the type of man who grovels well, Sabrina. This had to be your choice. You had to come to me."

She pressed her open lips to his. "I came," she said quietly.

"Ah, but does that mean yes?" he countered her. There was a world of waiting in his eyes.

"Yes?"

"You're not supposed to say it with a question mark after it. I'm asking you to stay in Houston for another few months and marry me."

She stared at him, fresh amazement sliding through her. "How can you doubt it?"

He lifted an eyebrow at her. "As I remember it, the last time we spoke about love, you couldn't give me a definitive answer."

A sigh slid from her as she remembered that afternoon. "I was afraid then," she answered softly.

"And now?"

She closed her eyes and took a deep breath. "I love you, Chase Cutter."

"Enough to stay here with me and not run back into hiding after a few months of civilization? We'll have to stay here until I finish this place. I can't start the marina development until then. Won't you miss your paradise?"

She looked up at him longingly. "I'm beginning to think that paradise is wherever you are. Thunder Cay wasn't the same without you."

He crushed her to him. Her whole being seemed to be filled with waiting until he finally broke the silence with the only words she needed to hear.

"I love you, Tiger Eyes," he whispered against her hair.

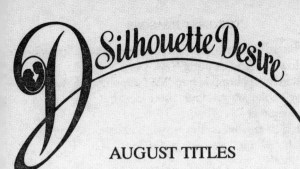

Silhouette Desire

AUGUST TITLES

THE DEVIL TO PAY
Stephanie James

THE TENDER BARBARIAN
Dixie Browning

STARSTRUCK LOVERS
Suzanne Michelle

THE BEST REASONS
Beverly Bird

CAPITOL AFFAIR
Fran Bergen

MORE THAN PROMISES
Amanda Lee

Silhouette Desire

COMING NEXT MONTH

A DIFFERENT REALITY
Nora Powers

It didn't take long before his dark eyes and whimsical imagination had her head spinning until she wasn't sure where the border between fantasy and reality lay. But while Kerr's fantasies were truly fantastic, his feelings were passionately real. Or were they…?

A WOMAN OF INTEGRITY
Marie Nicole

Chyna O'Brien was a stuntwoman, a professional risk taker. Maybe Matt really *did* feel something for her. Finding out was going to be the most dangerous move of her career.

GOLDEN MAN
Ann Major

Having Blade around stirred feelings Jenny feared. His golden looks and the vivid memory of an afternoon they'd once shared were enough to set her heart ablaze all over again…

 *Silhouette Desire*

COMING NEXT MONTH

CATTLEMAN'S CHOICE
Diana Palmer

No other woman dared approach him. And even
Mandelyn soon began to wonder whether a few
lessons in manners could ever make a gentleman of
an outlaw like Carson Wayne.

HUNGRY FOR LOVE
Ariel Berk

Wealthy, self-made, Wes was a curious mixture of
street tough and tender lover, straightforward…
honest. Though they came from opposite
backgrounds, they both had the same thing to prove,
the same needs: a hunger for love.

JOURNEY TO DESIRE
Laurie Paige

Tender, provocative Mark Terrington seemed bent
on learning her secrets, even as he remained
strangely distant. Had she fallen in love with the
man of her dreams, or a dangerous enemy who was
after her mind, not her heart?

Four New
Silhouette Romances
could be yours
ABSOLUTELY FREE

Did you know that Silhouette Romances are no longer available from the shops in the U.K?

Read on to discover how you could receive four brand new Silhouette Romances, **free** and **without obligation,** with this special introductory offer to the new Silhouette Reader Service.

As thousands of women who have read these books know — Silhouette Romances sweep you away into an exciting love filled world of fascination between men and women. A world filled with

age-old conflicts — love and money, ambition and guilt, jealousy and pride, even life and death.

Silhouette Romances are the latest stories written by the world's best romance writers, and they are **only** available from Silhouette Reader Service. Take out a subscription and you could receive 6 brand new titles every month, plus a newsletter bringing you all the latest information from Silhouette's New York editors. All this delivered in one exciting parcel direct to your door, with no charges for postage and packing.

And at only 95p for a book, Silhouette Romances represent the very best value in Romantic Reading.

Remember, Silhouette Romances are **only** available to subscribers, so don't miss out on this very special opportunity. Fill in the certificate below and post it today. You don't even need a stamp.

-- ✂ — — —

FREE BOOK CERTIFICATE

To: Silhouette Reader Service, FREEPOST, P.O. Box 236, Croydon, Surrey. CR9 9EL

Readers in South Africa—write to
Silhouette Romance Club, Private Bag X3010, Randburg 2125

Yes, please send me, free and without obligation, four brand new Silhouette Romances and reserve a subscription for me. If I decide to subscribe, I shall receive six brand new books every month for £5.70 , post and packing free. If I decide not to subscribe I shall write to you within 10 days The free books are mine to keep, whatever I decide. I understand that I may cancel my subscription at any time simply by writing to you. I am over 18 years of age. Please write in BLOCK CAPITALS

Signature _____

Name _____

Address _____

_____ Postcode _____

SEND NO MONEY — TAKE NO RISKS.
Please don't forget to include your Postcode.

Remember postcodes speed delivery Offer applies in U.K. only and is not valid to present subscribers Silhouette reserve the right to exercise discretion in granting membership If price changes are necessary you will be notified Offer expires December 1985.

EPS1

Silhouette Desire

Your chance to write back!

We'll send you details of an exciting free offer from *SILHOUETTE*, if you can help us by answering the few simple questions below.

Just fill in this questionnaire, tear it out and put it in an envelope and post today to: Silhouette Reader Survey, FREEPOST, P.O. Box 236, Croydon, Surrey CR9 9EL. You don't even need a stamp.

What is the title of the *SILHOUETTE* Desire you have just read?
_____

How much did you enjoy it?

Very much ☐   Quite a lot ☐   Not very much ☐

Would you buy another *SILHOUETTE* Desire book?

Yes ☐   Possibly ☐   No ☐

How did you discover *SILHOUETTE* Desire books?

Advertising ☐   A friend ☐   Seeing them on sale ☐

Elsewhere (please state) _____

How often do you read romantic fiction?

Frequently ☐   Occasionally ☐   Rarely ☐

Name (Mrs/Miss) _____

Address _____

_____

_____ Postcode _____

Age group: Under 24 ☐   25–34 ☐   35–44 ☐

45–55 ☐   Over 55 ☐

Silhouette Reader Service, P.O. Box 236, Croydon, Surrey CR9 9EL.
Readers in South Africa—write to:
Silhouette Romance Club,
Private Bag X3010, Randburg 2125.

SD1